SHERWOOD ANDERSON (1[...] and began his career at the age [...] and serving in the Spanish-Am[...] native state, was married, and m[...] one day when he walked out o[...] and made his way to Chicago. Th[...] ...ting advertising copy, he met such authors as Carl Sandburg and Floyd Dell, who encouraged him to publish his first book, *Windy McPherson's Son* (1916), a novel dealing with a boy's life in an Iowa town. His next novel, *Marching Men* (1917), was set in the Pennsylvania coal region. He also published a book of poems, *Mid-American Chants* (1918), but it was not until 1919, when *Winesburg, Ohio* appeared, that he first attracted wide attention. These stories of small-town people voice the philosophy of life expressed in all his later works.

The same themes and attitudes are expressed in subsequent books: *The Triumph of the Egg* (1921), stories and poems; *Horses and Men* (1923), stories mainly about horse racing; and *Many Marriages* (1923), a novel about a man's attempt to escape routine. In his novel *Dark Laughter* (1925), he reached artistic maturity both in his simple and direct style and in his mastery of form. Other books are *Poor White* (1920), *Tar: A Midwest Childhood* (1926), and *A Story Teller's Story* (1924).

After issuing two volumes of sketches, *The Modern Writer* (1925) and *Sherwood Anderson's Notebook* (1926), and a volume of poetry, *A New Testament* (1927), he retired to a small Virginia town to edit newspapers. His next book, *Hello Towns!* (1929), was a narrative of visits to small towns; *Nearer the Grass Roots* (1929) and *Perhaps Women* (1931) are nonfiction works. *Beyond Desire* (1932), his first novel in seven years, was concerned with problems of modern frustrations. *Death in the Woods* (1933), *Puzzled America* (1935), and *Kit Brandon* (1936) show the author's characters still trapped in situations in which they cannot cope. *Home Town* (1940) is a collection of essays. *Memoirs* (1942) and *Letters* (1953) were issued posthumously.

DEATH IN THE WOODS

DEATH IN THE
WOODS
AND OTHER STORIES

SHERWOOD
ANDERSON

SHORELINE BOOKS

an imprint of
W · W · NORTON & COMPANY · NEW YORK · LONDON

Published simultaneously in Canada by Penguin Books Canada Ltd,
2801 John Street, Markham, Ontario L3R 1B4

Printed in the United States of America.

ISBN 0-87140-140-1

W. W. Norton & Company, Inc., 500 Fifth Avenue, New York, N.Y. 10110
W. W. Norton & Company Ltd., 37 Great Russell Street, London WC1B 3NU

1 2 3 4 5 6 7 8 9 0

TO MY FRIEND

FERDINAND SCHEVILL

CONTENTS

DEATH IN THE
WOODS

DEATH IN THE WOODS

S H E was an old woman and lived on a farm near the town in which I lived. All country and small-town people have seen such old women, but no one knows much about them. Such an old woman comes into town driving an old worn-out horse or she comes afoot carrying a basket. She may own a few hens and have eggs to sell. She brings them in a basket and takes them to a grocer. There she trades them in. She gets some salt pork and some beans. Then she gets a pound or two of sugar and some flour.

Afterwards she goes to the butcher's and asks for some dog-meat. She may spend ten or fifteen cents, but when she does she asks for something. Formerly the butchers gave liver to any one who wanted to carry it away. In our family we were always having it. Once one of my brothers got a whole cow's liver at the slaughter-house near the fair-grounds in our town. We had it until we were sick of it. It never cost a cent. I have hated the thought of it ever since.

The old farm woman got some liver and a soup-bone. She never visited with any one, and as soon as she got what she wanted she lit out for home. It made quite a load for such an old body. No one gave her a lift. People drive right down a road and never notice an old woman like that.

There was such an old woman who used to come into town past our house one Summer and Fall when I was a young boy and was sick with what was called inflammatory rheumatism. She went home later carrying a heavy pack on her back. Two or three large gaunt-looking dogs followed at her heels.

The old woman was nothing special. She was one of the nameless ones that hardly any one knows, but she got into my thoughts. I have just suddenly now, after all these years, remembered her and what happened. It is a story. Her name was Grimes, and she lived with her husband and son in a small un-painted house on the bank of a small creek four miles from town.

The husband and son were a tough lot. Although the son was but twenty-one, he had already served a term in jail. It was whispered about that the woman's husband stole horses and ran them off to some other county. Now and then, when a horse turned up missing, the man had also disappeared. No one ever caught him. Once, when I was loafing at Tom Whitehead's livery-barn, the man came there and sat on the bench in front. Two or three other men were there, but no one spoke to him. He sat for a few minutes and then got up and went away. When he was leaving he turned around and stared at the men. There was a look of defiance in his eyes. "Well, I have tried to be friendly. You don't want to talk to me. It has been so wherever I have gone in this town. If, some day, one of your fine horses turns up missing, well, then what?" He did not say anything actually. "I'd like to bust one of you on the jaw," was about what his eyes said. I remember how the look in his eyes made me shiver.

The old man belonged to a family that had had money once. His name was Jake Grimes. It all comes back clearly now. His father, John Grimes, had owned a sawmill when the country was new, and had made money. Then he got to drinking and running after women. When he died there wasn't much left.

Jake blew in the rest. Pretty soon there wasn't any more lumber to cut and his land was nearly all gone.

He got his wife off a German farmer, for whom he went to work one June day in the wheat harvest. She was a young thing then and scared to death. You see, the farmer was up to something with the girl—she was, I think, a bound girl and his wife had her suspicions. She took it out on the girl when the man wasn't around. Then, when the wife had to go off to town for supplies, the farmer got after her. She told young Jake that nothing really ever happened, but he didn't know whether to believe it or not.

He got her pretty easy himself, the first time he was out with her. He wouldn't have married her if the German farmer hadn't tried to tell him where to get off. He got her to go riding with him in his buggy one night when he was threshing on the place, and then he came for her the next Sunday night.

She managed to get out of the house without her employer's seeing, but when she was getting into the buggy he showed up. It was almost dark, and he just popped up suddenly at the horse's head. He grabbed the horse by the bridle and Jake got out his buggy-whip.

They had it out all right! The German was a tough one. Maybe he didn't care whether his wife knew or not. Jake hit him over the face and shoulders with the buggy-whip, but the horse got to acting up and he had to get out.

Then the two men went for it. The girl didn't see it. The horse started to run away and went nearly a mile down the road before the girl got him stopped. Then she managed to tie him to a tree beside the road. (I wonder how I know all this. It must have stuck in my mind from small-town tales when I was a boy.) Jake found her there after he got through with the German. She was huddled up in the buggy seat, crying, scared to death. She told Jake a lot of stuff, how the German had tried to get her, how he chased her once into the barn, how another time, when they happened to be alone in the house together, he tore her dress open clear down the front. The German, she said, might have got her that time if he hadn't heard his old woman drive in at the gate. She had been off to town for supplies. Well, she would be putting the horse in the barn. The German managed to sneak off to the fields without his wife seeing. He told the girl he would kill her if she told. What could she do? She told a lie about ripping her dress in the barn when she was feeding the stock. I remember now that she was a bound girl and did not know where her father and mother were. Maybe she did not have any father. You know what I mean.

Such bound children were often enough cruelly treated. They were children who had no parents, slaves really. There were very few orphan homes then. They were legally bound into some home. It was a matter of pure luck how it came out.

II

S H E married Jake and had a son and daughter, but the daughter died.

Then she settled down to feed stock. That was her job. At the German's place she had cooked the food for the German and his wife. The wife was a strong woman with big hips and worked most of the time in the fields with her husband. She fed them and fed the cows in the barn, fed the pigs, the horses and the chickens. Every moment of every day, as a young girl, was spent feeding something.

Then she married Jake Grimes and he had to be fed. She was a slight thing, and when she had been married for three or four years, and after the two children were born, her slender shoulders became stooped.

Jake always had a lot of big dogs around the house, that stood near the unused sawmill near the creek. He was always trading horses when he wasn't stealing something and had a lot of poor bony ones about. Also he kept three or four pigs and a cow. They were all pastured in the few acres left of the Grimes place and Jake did little enough work.

He went into debt for a threshing outfit and ran it for several years, but it did not pay. People did

8

not trust him. They were afraid he would steal the grain at night. He had to go a long way off to get work and it cost too much to get there. In the Winter he hunted and cut a little firewood, to be sold in some nearby town. When the son grew up he was just like the father. They got drunk together. If there wasn't anything to eat in the house when they came home the old man gave his old woman a cut over the head. She had a few chickens of her own and had to kill one of them in a hurry. When they were all killed she wouldn't have any eggs to sell when she went to town, and then what would she do?

She had to scheme all her life about getting things fed, getting the pigs fed so they would grow fat and could be butchered in the Fall. When they were butchered her husband took most of the meat off to town and sold it. If he did not do it first the boy did. They fought sometimes and when they fought the old woman stood aside trembling.

She had got the habit of silence anyway—that was fixed. Sometimes, when she began to look old— she wasn't forty yet—and when the husband and son were both off, trading horses or drinking or hunting or stealing, she went around the house and the barnyard muttering to herself.

How was she going to get everything fed?—that was her problem. The dogs had to be fed. There wasn't enough hay in the barn for the horses and the cow. If she didn't feed the chickens how could they lay eggs? Without eggs to sell how could she get things in town, things she had to have to keep the life of the farm going? Thank heaven, she did not have to feed her husband—in a certain way. That hadn't lasted long after their marriage and after the babies came. Where he went on his long trips she did not know. Sometimes he was gone from home for weeks, and after the boy grew up they went off together.

They left everything at home for her to manage and she had no money. She knew no one. No one ever talked to her in town. When it was Winter she had to gather sticks of wood for her fire, had to try to keep the stock fed with very little grain.

The stock in the barn cried to her hungrily, the dogs followed her about. In the Winter the hens laid few enough eggs. They huddled in the corners of the barn and she kept watching them. If a hen lays an egg in the barn in the Winter and you do not find it, it freezes and breaks.

One day in Winter the old woman went off to town with a few eggs and the dogs followed her. She did not get started until nearly three o'clock and the snow was heavy. She hadn't been feeling very well for several days and so she went muttering along, scantily clad, her shoulders stooped. She had an old grain bag in which she carried her eggs, tucked away down in the bottom. There weren't many of them, but in Winter the price of eggs is up. She would get a little meat in exchange for the eggs, some salt pork, a little sugar, and some coffee perhaps. It might be the butcher would give her a piece of liver.

When she had got to town and was trading in her eggs the dogs lay by the door outside. She did pretty well, got the things she needed, more than she had hoped. Then she went to the butcher and he gave her some liver and some dog-meat.

It was the first time any one had spoken to her in a friendly way for a long time. The butcher was alone in his shop when she came in and was annoyed by the thought of such a sick-looking old woman out on such a day. It was bitter cold and the snow, that had let up during the afternoon, was falling again. The butcher said something about her husband and her son, swore at them, and the old woman stared at him, a look of mild surprise in her eyes as he talked. He said that if either the husband or the son were going to get any of the liver or the heavy bones with scraps of meat hanging to them that he had put into the grain bag, he'd see him starve first.

Starve, eh? Well, things had to be fed. Men had

11

to be fed, and the horses that weren't any good but maybe could be traded off, and the poor thin cow that hadn't given any milk for three months.

Horses, cows, pigs, dogs, men.

III

THE old woman had to get back before darkness came if she could. The dogs followed at her heels, sniffing at the heavy grain bag she had fastened on her back. When she got to the edge of town she stopped by a fence and tied the bag on her back with a piece of rope she had carried in her dress-pocket for just that purpose. That was an easier way to carry it. Her arms ached. It was hard when she had to crawl over fences and once she fell over and landed in the snow. The dogs went frisking about. She had to struggle to get to her feet again, but she made it. The point of climbing over the fences was that there was a short cut over a hill and through a woods. She might have gone around by the road, but it was a mile farther that way. She was afraid she couldn't make it. And then, besides, the stock had to be fed. There was a little hay left and a little corn. Perhaps her husband and son would bring some home when they came. They had driven off in the only buggy the Grimes family had, a rickety thing, a rickety horse hitched to the buggy, two other rickety horses led by halters. They were going to trade horses, get a little money if they could. They might come home drunk. It would be well to have something in the house when they came back.

The son had an affair on with a woman at the county seat, fifteen miles away. She was a rough enough woman, a tough one. Once, in the Summer, the son had brought her to the house. Both she and the son had been drinking. Jake Grimes was away and the son and his woman ordered the old woman about like a servant. She didn't mind much; she was used to it. Whatever happened she never said anything. That was her way of getting along. She had managed that way when she was a young girl at the German's and ever since she had married Jake. That time her son brought his woman to the house they stayed all night, sleeping together just as though they were married. It hadn't shocked the old woman, not much. She had got past being shocked early in life.

With the pack on her back she went painfully along across an open field, wading in the deep snow, and got into the woods.

There was a path, but it was hard to follow. Just beyond the top of the hill, where the woods was thickest, there was a small clearing. Had some one once thought of building a house there? The clearing was as large as a building lot in town, large enough for a house and a garden. The path ran along the side of the clearing, and when she got there the old woman sat down to rest at the foot of a tree.

It was a foolish thing to do. When she got herself placed, the pack against the tree's trunk, it was nice, but what about getting up again? She worried about that for a moment and then quietly closed her eyes.

She must have slept for a time. When you are about so cold you can't get any colder. The afternoon grew a little warmer and the snow came thicker than ever. Then after a time the weather cleared. The moon even came out.

There were four Grimes dogs that had followed Mrs. Grimes into town, all tall gaunt fellows. Such men as Jake Grimes and his son always keep just such dogs. They kick and abuse them, but they stay. The Grimes dogs, in order to keep from starving, had to do a lot of foraging for themselves, and they had been at it while the old woman slept with her back to the tree at the side of the clearing. They had been chasing rabbits in the woods and in adjoining fields and in their ranging had picked up three other farm dogs.

After a time all the dogs came back to the clearing. They were excited about something. Such

14

nights, cold and clear and with a moon, do things to dogs. It may be that some old instinct, come down from the time when they were wolves and ranged the woods in packs on Winter nights, comes back into them.

The dogs in the clearing, before the old woman, had caught two or three rabbits and their immediate hunger had been satisfied. They began to play, running in circles in the clearing. Round and round they ran, each dog's nose at the tail of the next dog. In the clearing, under the snow-laden trees and under the wintry moon they made a strange picture, running thus silently, in a circle their running had beaten in the soft snow. The dogs made no sound. They ran around and around in the circle.

It may have been that the old woman saw them doing that before she died. She may have awakened once or twice and looked at the strange sight with dim old eyes.

She wouldn't be very cold now, just drowsy. Life hangs on a long time. Perhaps the old woman was out of her head. She may have dreamed of her girlhood, at the German's, and before that, when she was a child and before her mother lit out and left her.

Her dreams couldn't have been very pleasant. Not many pleasant things had happened to her. Now and then one of the Grimes dogs left the running circle and came to stand before her. The dog thrust his face close to her face. His red tongue was hanging out.

The running of the dogs may have been a kind of death ceremony. It may have been that the primitive instinct of the wolf, having been aroused in the dogs by the night and the running, made them somehow afraid.

"Now we are no longer wolves. We are dogs, the servants of men. Keep alive, man! When man dies we becomes wolves again."

When one of the dogs came to where the old woman sat with her back against the tree and thrust his nose close to her face he seemed satisfied and went back to run with the pack. All the Grimes dogs did it at some time during the evening, before she died. I knew all about it afterward, when I grew to be a man, because once in a woods in Illinois, on another Winter night, I saw a pack of dogs act just like that. The dogs were waiting for me to die as they had waited for the old woman that night when I was a child, but when it happened to me I was a young man and had no intention whatever of dying.

The old woman died softly and quietly. When she was dead and when one of the Grimes dogs had come to her and had found her dead all the dogs stopped running.

16

They gathered about her.

Well, she was dead now. She had fed the Grimes dogs when she was alive, what about now?

There was the pack on her back, the grain bag containing the piece of salt pork, the liver the butcher had given her, the dog-meat, the soup bones. The butcher in town, having been suddenly overcome with a feeling of pity, had loaded her grain bag heavily. It had been a big haul for the old woman.

It was a big haul for the dogs now.

IV

ONE of the Grimes dogs sprang suddenly out from among the others and began worrying the pack on the old woman's back. Had the dogs really been wolves that one would have been the leader of the pack. What he did, all the others did.

All of them sank their teeth into the grain bag the old woman had fastened with ropes to her back.

They dragged the old woman's body out into the open clearing. The worn-out dress was quickly torn from her shoulders. When she was found, a day or two later, the dress had been torn from her body clear to the hips, but the dogs had not touched her body. They had got the meat out of the grain

17

bag, that was all. Her body was frozen stiff when it was found, and the shoulders were so narrow and the body so slight that in death it looked like the body of some charming young girl.

Such things happened in towns of the Middle West, on farms near town, when I was a boy. A hunter out after rabbits found the old woman's body and did not touch it. Something, the beaten round path in the little snow-covered clearing, the silence of the place, the place where the dogs had worried the body trying to pull the grain bag away or tear it open—something startled the man and he hurried off to town.

I was in Main street with one of my brothers who was town newsboy and who was taking the afternoon papers to the stores. It was almost night.

The hunter came into a grocery and told his story. Then he went to a hardware-shop and into a drugstore. Men began to gather on the sidewalks. Then they started out along the road to the place in the woods.

My brother should have gone on about his business of distributing papers but he didn't. Every one was going to the woods. The undertaker went and the town marshal. Several men got on a dray and rode out to where the path left the road and went into the woods, but the horses weren't very sharply shod and slid about on the slippery roads. They made no better time than those of us who walked.

The town marshal was a large man whose leg had been injured in the Civil War. He carried a heavy cane and limped rapidly along the road. My brother and I followed at his heels, and as we went other men and boys joined the crowd.

It had grown dark by the time we got to where the old woman had left the road but the moon had come out. The marshal was thinking there might have been a murder. He kept asking the hunter questions. The hunter went along with his gun across his shoulders, a dog following at his heels. It isn't often a rabbit hunter has a chance to be so conspicuous. He was taking full advantage of it, leading the procession with the town marshal. "I didn't see any wounds. She was a beautiful young girl. Her face was buried in the snow. No, I didn't know her." As a matter of fact, the hunter had not looked closely at the body. He had been frightened. She might have been murdered and some one might spring out from behind a tree and murder him. In a woods, in the late afternoon, when the trees are all bare and there is white snow on the ground, when all is silent, something creepy steals over the mind and body. If something strange or uncanny has happened in the neighborhood all you think about is getting away from there as fast as you can.

The crowd of men and boys had got to where the old woman had crossed the field and went, following the marshal and the hunter, up the slight incline and into the woods.

My brother and I were silent. He had his bundle of papers in a bag slung across his shoulder. When he got back to town he would have to go on distributing his papers before he went home to supper. If I went along, as he had no doubt already determined I should, we would both be late. Either mother or our older sister would have to warm our supper.

Well, we would have something to tell. A boy did not get such a chance very often. It was lucky we just happened to go into the grocery when the hunter came in. The hunter was a country fellow. Neither of us had ever seen him before.

Now the crowd of men and boys had got to the clearing. Darkness comes quickly on such Winter nights, but the full moon made everything clear. My brother and I stood near the tree, beneath which the old woman had died.

She did not look old, lying there in that light, frozen and still. One of the men turned her over in the snow and I saw everything. My body trembled with some strange mystical feeling and so did my brother's. It might have been the cold.

Neither of us had ever seen a woman's body before. It may have been the snow, clinging to the frozen flesh, that made it look so white and lovely, so like marble. No woman had come with the party from town; but one of the men, he was the town blacksmith, took off his overcoat and spread it over her. Then he gathered her into his arms and started off to town, all the others following silently. At that time no one knew who she was.

V

I HAD seen everything, had seen the oval in the snow, like a miniature race-track, where the dogs had run, had seen how the men were mystified, had seen the white bare young-looking shoulders, had heard the whispered comments of the men.

The men were simply mystified. They took the body to the undertaker's, and when the blacksmith, the hunter, the marshal and several others had got inside they closed the door. If father had been there perhaps he could have got in, but we boys couldn't.

I went with my brother to distribute the rest of his papers and when we got home it was my brother who told the story.

I kept silent and went to bed early. It may have been I was not satisfied with the way he told it.

Later, in the town, I must have heard other fragments of the old woman's story. She was recognized the next day and there was an investigation.

The husband and son were found somewhere and brought to town and there was an attempt to connect them with the woman's death, but it did not work. They had perfect enough alibis.

However, the town was against them. They had to get out. Where they went I never heard.

I remember only the picture there in the forest, the men standing about, the naked girlish-looking figure, face down in the snow, the tracks made by the running dogs and the clear cold Winter sky above. White fragments of clouds were drifting across the sky. They went racing across the little open space among the trees.

The scene in the forest had become for me, without my knowing it, the foundation for the real story I am now trying to tell. The fragments, you see, had to be picked up slowly, long afterwards.

Things happened. When I was a young man I worked on the farm of a German. The hired-girl was afraid of her employer. The farmer's wife hated her.

I saw things at that place. Once later, I had a half-uncanny, mystical adventure with dogs in an

Illinois forest on a clear, moon-lit Winter night. When I was a schoolboy, and on a Summer day, I went with a boy friend out along a creek some miles from town and came to the house where the old woman had lived. No one had lived in the house since her death. The doors were broken from the hinges; the window lights were all broken. As the boy and I stood in the road outside, two dogs, just roving farm dogs no doubt, came running around the corner of the house. The dogs were tall, gaunt fellows and came down to the fence and glared through at us, standing in the road.

The whole thing, the story of the old woman's death, was to me as I grew older like music heard from far off. The notes had to be picked up slowly one at a time. Something had to be understood.

The woman who died was one destined to feed animal life. Anyway, that is all she ever did. She was feeding animal life before she was born, as a child, as a young woman working on the farm of the German, after she married, when she grew old and when she died. She fed animal life in cows, in chickens, in pigs, in horses, in dogs, in men. Her daughter had died in childhood and with her one son she had no articulate relations. On the night when she died she was hurrying homeward, bearing on her body food for animal life.

She died in the clearing in the woods and even after her death continued feeding animal life.

You see it is likely that, when my brother told the story, that night when we got home and my mother and sister sat listening, I did not think he got the point. He was too young and so was I. A thing so complete has its own beauty.

I shall not try to emphasize the point. I am only explaining why I was dissatisfied then and have been ever since. I speak of that only that you may understand why I have been impelled to try to tell the simple story over again.

THE RETURN

THE RETURN

EIGHTEEN years. Well, he was driving a good car, an expensive roadster. He was well clad, a rather solid, fine-looking man, not too heavy. When he had left the Middle-Western town to go live in New York City he was twenty-two and now, on his way back, he was forty. He drove toward the town from the east, stopping for lunch at another town ten miles away.

When he went away from Caxton, after his mother died, he used to write letters to friends at home, but after several months the replies began to come with less and less frequency. On the day when he sat eating his lunch at a small hotel in the town ten miles east of Caxton he suddenly thought of the reason, and was ashamed. "Am I going back there on this visit for the same reason I wrote the letters?" he asked himself. For a moment he thought he might not go on. There was still time to turn back.

Outside, in the principal business street of the neighboring town, people were walking about. The sun shone warmly. Although he had lived for so many years in New York, he had always kept, buried away in him somewhere, a hankering for his own country. All the day before he had been driving through the Eastern Ohio country, crossing many small streams, running down through small valleys, seeing the white farmhouses set back from the road, and the big red barns.

The elders were still in bloom along the fences, boys were swimming in a creek, the wheat had been cut, and now the corn was shoulder-high. Everywhere the drone of bees; in patches of woodland along the road, a heavy, mysterious silence.

Now, however, he began thinking of something else. Shame crept over him. "When I first left Caxton, I wrote letters back to my boyhood friends there, but I wrote always of myself. When I had written a letter telling what I was doing in the city, what friends I was making, what my prospects were, I put, at the very end of the letter, perhaps, a little inquiry: 'I hope you are well. How are things going with you?' Something of that sort."

The returning native—his name was John Holden—had grown very uneasy. After eighteen years it seemed to him he could see, lying before him, one of the letters written eighteen years before, when he had first come into the strange Eastern city. His mother's brother, a successful architect in the city, had given him such and such an opportunity: he had been at the theater to see Mansfield as Brutus; he had taken the night boat up-river to Albany with his aunt; there were two very handsome girls on the boat.

Everything must have been in the same tone. His uncle had given him a rare opportunity, and he had taken advantage of it. In time he had also become a successful architect. In New York City there were certain great buildings, two or three skyscrapers, several huge industrial plants, any number of handsome and expensive residences, that were the products of his brain.

When it came down to scratch, John Holden had to admit that his uncle had not been excessively fond of him. It had just happened that his aunt and uncle had no children of their own. He did his work in the office well and carefully, had developed a certain rather striking knack for design. The aunt had liked him better. She had always tried to think of him as her own son, had treated him as a son. Sometimes she called him son. Once or twice, after his uncle died, he had a notion. His aunt was a good woman, but sometimes he thought she would rather have enjoyed having him, John Holden, go in a bit more for wickedness, go a little on the loose, now and then. He never did anything she had to forgive him for. Perhaps she hungered for the opportunity to forgive.

Odd thoughts, eh? Well, what was a fellow to do? You had but the one life to live. You had to think of yourself.

Botheration! John Holden had rather counted on the trip back to Caxton, had really counted on it more than he realized. It was a bright Summer day. He had been driving over the mountains of Pennsylvania, through New York State, through Eastern Ohio. Gertrude, his wife, had died during the Summer before, and his one son, a lad of twelve, had gone away for the Summer to a boys' camp in Vermont.

The idea had just come to him. "I'll drive the car along slowly through the country, drinking it in. I need a rest, time to think. What I really need is to renew old acquaintances. I'll go back to Caxton and stay several days. I'll see Herman and Frank and Joe. Then I'll go call on Lillian and Kate. What a lot of fun, really!" It might just be that when he got to Caxton, the Caxton ball team would be playing a game, say with a team from Yerington. Lillian might go to the game with him. It was in his mind faintly that Lillian had never married. How did he know that? He had heard nothing from Caxton for many years. The ball game would be in Heffler's field, and he and Lillian would go out there, walking under the maple trees along Turner Street, past the old stave factory, then in the dust of the road, past where the sawmill used to stand, and on into the field itself. He would be carrying a sunshade over Lillian's head, and Bob French would be standing at the gate where you went into the field and charging the people twenty-five cents to see the game.

Well, it would not be Bob; his son, perhaps. There would be something very nice in the notion of Lillian's going off to a ball game that way with an old sweetheart. A crowd of boys, women and men, going through a cattle gate into Heffler's field, tramping through the dust, young men with their sweethearts, a few gray-haired women, mothers of boys who belonged to the team, Lillian and he sitting in the rickety grandstand in the hot sun.

Once it had been—how they had felt, he and Lillian, sitting there together! It had been rather hard to keep the attention centered on the players in the field. One couldn't ask a neighbor, "Who's ahead now, Caxton or Yerington?" Lillian's hands lay in her lap. What white, delicate, expressive hands they were! Once—that was just before he went away to live in the city with his uncle and but a month after his mother died—he and Lillian went to the ball field together at night. His father had died when he was a young lad, and he had no relatives left in the town. Going off to the ball field at night was maybe a risky thing for Lillian to do—risky for her reputation if any one found it out—but she had seemed willing enough. You know how small-town girls of that age are.

Her father owned a retail shoe store in Caxton, and was a good, respectable man; but the Holdens —John's father had been a lawyer.

After they got back from the ball field that night —it must have been after midnight—they went to sit on the front porch before her father's house. He must have known. A daughter cavorting about half the night with a young man that way! They had clung to each other with a sort of queer, desperate feeling neither understood. She did not go into the house until after three o'clock, and went then only because he insisted. He hadn't wanted to ruin her reputation. Why, he might have . . . She was like a little frightened child at the thought of his going away. He was twenty-two then, and she must have been about eighteen.

Eighteen and twenty-two make forty. John Holden was forty on the day when he sat at lunch at the hotel in the town ten miles from Caxton.

Now, he thought, he might be able to walk through the streets of Caxton to the ball park with

Lillian with a certain effect. You know how it is. One has to accept the fact that youth is gone. If there should turn out to be such a ball game and Lillian would go with him, he would leave the car in the garage and ask her to walk. One saw pictures of that sort of thing in the movies—a man coming back to his native village after twenty years; a new beauty taking the place of the beauty of youth—something like that. In the Spring the leaves on maple trees are lovely, but they are even more lovely in the Fall —a flame of color—manhood and womanhood.

After he had finished his lunch John did not feel very comfortable. The road to Caxton—it used to take nearly three hours to travel the distance with a horse and buggy, but now, and without any effort, the distance might be made in twenty minutes.

He lit a cigar and went for a walk, not in the streets of Caxton, but in the streets of the town ten miles away. If he got to Caxton in the evening, just at dusk, say, now . . .

With an inward pang John realized that he wanted darkness, the kindliness of soft evening lights. Lillian, Joe, Herman and the rest. It had been eighteen years for the others as well as for himself. Now he had succeeded, a little, in twisting his fear of Caxton into fear for the others, and it made him feel somewhat better; but at once he realized what he was doing and again felt uncomfortable. One had to look out for changes, new people, new buildings, middle-aged people grown old, youth grown middle-aged. At any rate, he was thinking of the other now. He wasn't, as when he wrote letters home eighteen years before, thinking only of himself. "Am I?" It *was* a question.

An absurd situation, really. He had sailed along so gayly through upper New York State, through Western Pennsylvania, through Eastern Ohio. Men were at work in the fields and in the towns, farmers drove into towns in their cars, clouds of dust rose on some distant road, seen across a valley. Once he had stopped his car near a bridge and had gone for a walk along the banks of a creek where it wound through a wood.

He was liking people. Well, he had never before given much time to people, to thinking of them and their affairs. "I hadn't time," he told himself. He had always realized that, while he was a good enough architect, things move fast in America. New men were coming on. He couldn't take chances of going on forever on his uncle's reputation. A man had to be always on the alert. Fortunately, his marriage had been a help. It had made valuable connections for him.

Twice he had picked up people on the road.

There was a lad of sixteen from some town of Eastern Pennsylvania, working his way westward toward the Pacific Coast by picking up rides in cars—a Summer's adventure. John had carried him all of one day and had listened to his talk with keen pleasure. And so this was the younger generation. The boy had nice eyes and an eager, friendly manner. He smoked cigarettes, and once, when they had a puncture, he was very quick and eager about changing the tire. "Now, don't you soil your hands, Mister, I can do it like a flash," he said, and he did. The boy said he intended working his way overland to the Pacific Coast, where he would try to get a job of some kind on an ocean freighter, and that, if he did, he would go on around the world. "But do you speak any foreign languages?" The boy did not. Across John Holden's mind flashed pictures of hot Eastern deserts, crowded Asiatic towns, wild half-savage mountain countries. As a young architect, and before his uncle died, he had spent two years in foreign travel, studying buildings in many countries; but he said nothing of this thought to the boy. Vast plans entered into with eager, boyish abandon, a world tour undertaken as he, when a young man, might have undertaken to find his way from his uncle's house in East Eighty-first Street downtown to the Battery. "How do I know—perhaps he will do it?" John thought.

The day in company with the boy had been very pleasant, and he had been on the alert to pick him up again the next morning; but the boy had gone on his way, had caught a ride with some earlier riser. Why hadn't John invited him to his hotel for the night? The notion hadn't come to him until too late.

Youth, rather wild and undisciplined, running wild, eh? I wonder why I never did it, never wanted to do it.

If he had been a bit wilder, more reckless—that night, that time when he and Lillian . . . "It's all right being reckless with yourself, but when some one else is involved, a young girl in a small town, you yourself lighting out . . ." He remembered sharply that on the night, long before, as he sat with Lillian on the porch before her father's house, his hand . . . It had seemed as though Lillian, on that evening, might not have objected to anything he wanted to do. He had thought—well, he had thought of the consequences. Women must be protected by men, all that sort of thing. Lillian had seemed rather stunned when he walked away, even though it was three o'clock in the morning. She had been rather like a person waiting at a railroad station for the coming of a train. There is a blackboard, and a strange man comes out and writes on it, "Train Number 287 has been discontinued"—something like that.

36

Well, it had been all right.

Later, four years later, he had married a New York woman of good family. Even in a city like New York, where there are so many people, her family had been well known. They had connections.

After marriage, sometimes, it is true, he had wondered. Gertrude used to look at him sometimes with an odd light in her eyes. That boy he picked up in the road—once during the day when he said something to the boy, the same queer look came into his eyes. It would be rather upsetting if you knew that the boy had purposely avoided you next morning. There had been Gertrude's cousin. Once after his marriage, John heard a rumor that Gertrude had wanted to marry that cousin, but of course he had said nothing to her. Why should he have? She was his wife. There had been, he had heard, a good deal of family objection to the cousin. He was reputed to be wild, a gambler and drinker.

Once the cousin came to the Holden apartment at two in the morning, drunk and demanding that he be allowed to see Gertrude, and she slipped on a dressing-gown and went down to him. That was in the hallway of the apartment, downstairs, where almost any one might have come in and seen her. As a matter of fact, the elevator boy and janitor did see her. She had stood in the hallway below talking

37

for nearly an hour. What about? He had never asked
Gertrude directly, and she had never told him anything. When she came upstairs again and had got
into her bed, he lay in his own bed trembling, but
remained silent. He had been afraid that if he spoke
he might say something rude; better keep still. The
cousin had disappeared. John had a suspicion that
Gertrude later supplied him with money. He went
out West somewhere.

Now Gertrude was dead. She had always seemed
very well, but suddenly she was attacked by a baf-
fling kind of slow fever that lasted nearly a year.
Sometimes she seemed about to get better, and then
suddenly the fever grew worse. It might be that she
did not want to live. What a notion! John had been
at the bedside with the doctor when she died. There
was something of the same feeling he had that night
of his youth when he went with Lillian to the ball
field, an odd sense of inadequacy. There was no
doubt that in some subtle way both women had
accused him.

Of what? There had always been, in some vague,
indefinable way, a kind of accusation in the attitude
toward him of his uncle, the architect, and of his
aunt. They had left him their money, but . . . It was
as though the uncle had said, as though Lillian during that night long ago had said . . .

Had they all said the same thing, and was Gertrude his wife saying it as she lay dying? A smile. "You have always taken such good care of yourself, haven't you, John dear? You have observed the rules. You have taken no chances for yourself or the others." She had actually said something of that sort to him once in a moment of anger.

II

In the small town ten miles from Caxton there wasn't any park to which a man could go to sit. If one stayed about the hotel, some one from Caxton might come in. "Hello, what are you doing here?"

It would be inconvenient to explain. He had wanted the kindliness of soft evening light, both for himself and the old friends he was to see again.

He began thinking of his son, now a boy of twelve. "Well," he said to himself, "his character has not begun to form yet." There was, as yet, in the son, an unconsciousness of other people, a rather casual selfishness, an unawareness of others, an unhealthy sharpness about getting the best of others. It was a thing that should be corrected in him and at once. John Holden had got himself into a small panic. "I must write him a letter at once. Such a habit gets fixed in a boy and then in the man, and it cannot later be shaken off. There are such a lot of people living in the world! Every man and woman has his own point of view. To be civilized, really, is to be aware of the others, their hopes, their gladnesses, their illusions about life."

John Holden was now walking along a residence street of a small Ohio town, composing in fancy a letter to his son in the boys' camp in Vermont. He was a man who wrote to his son every day. "I think a man should," he told himself. "He should remember that now the boy has no mother."

He had come to an outlying railroad station. It was neat with grass and flowers growing in a round bed in the very center of a lawn. Some man, the station agent and telegraph operator perhaps, passed him and went inside the station. John followed him in. On the wall of the waiting-room there was a framed copy of the time-table, and he stood studying it. A train went to Caxton at five. Another train came from Caxton and passed through the town he was now in at seven forty-three, the seven-nineteen out of Caxton. The man in the small business section of the station opened a sliding-panel and looked at him. The two men just stared at each other without speaking, and then the panel was slid shut again.

John looked at his watch. Two twenty-eight. At about six he could drive over to Caxton and dine at the hotel there. After he had dined, it would be evening and people would be coming into the main street. The seven-nineteen would come in. When John was a lad, sometimes, he, Joe, Herman, and often several other lads had climbed on the front of the baggage or mail car and had stolen a ride to the very town he was now in. What a thrill, crouched down in the gathering darkness on the platform as the train ran the ten miles, the car rocking from side to side! When it got a little dark, in the Fall or Spring, the fields beside the track were lighted up when the fireman opened his fire box to throw in coal. Once John saw a rabbit running along in the glare of light beside the track. He could have reached down and caught it with his hand. In the neighboring town the boys went into saloons and played pool and drank beer. They could depend upon catching a ride back home on the local freight that got to Caxton at about ten thirty. On one of the adventures John and Herman got drunk and Joe had to help them into an empty coal car and later get them out at Caxton. Herman got sick, and when they were getting off the freight at Caxton, he stumbled and came very near falling under the wheels of the moving train. John wasn't as drunk as Herman. When the others weren't looking, he had poured several of the glasses of beer into a spittoon.

In Caxton he and Joe had to walk about with Herman for several hours and when John finally got home, his mother was still awake and was worried. He had to lie to her. "I drove out into the country with Herman, and a wheel broke. We had to walk home." The reason Joe could carry his beer so well was because he was German. His father owned the town meat market and the family had beer on the table at home. No wonder it did not knock him out as it did Herman and John.

There was a bench at the side of the railroad station, in the shade, and John sat there for a long time—two hours, three hours. Why hadn't he brought a book? In fancy he composed a letter to his son and in it he spoke of the fields lying beside the road outside the town of Caxton, of his greeting old friends there, of things that had happened when he was a boy. He even spoke of his former sweetheart, of Lillian. If he now thought out just what he was going to say in the letter, he could write it in his room at the hotel over in Caxton in a few minutes without having to stop and think what he was going to say. You can't always be too fussy about what you say to a young boy. Really, sometimes, you should take him into your confidence, into your life, make him a part of your life.

It was six twenty when John drove into Caxton

and went to the hotel, where he registered, and was shown to a room. On the streets as he drove into town he saw Billy Baker, who, when he was a young man, had a paralyzed leg that dragged along the sidewalk when he walked. Now he was getting old; his face seemed wrinkled and faded, like a dried lemon, and his clothes had spots down the front. People, even sick people, live a long time in small Ohio towns. It is surprising how they hang on.

John had put his car, of a rather expensive make, into a garage beside the hotel. Formerly, in his day, the building had been used as a livery barn. There used to be pictures of famous trotting and pacing horses on the walls of the little office at the front. Old Dave Grey, who owned race horses of his own, ran the livery barn then, and John occasionally hired a rig there. He hired a rig and took Lillian for a ride into the country, along moonlit roads. By a lonely farmhouse a dog barked. Sometimes they drove along a little dirt road lined with elders and stopped the horse. How still everything was! What a queer feeling they had! They couldn't talk. Sometimes they sat in silence thus, very near each other, for a long, long time. Once they got out of the buggy, having tied the horse to the fence, and walked in a newly cut hay field. The cut hay lay all about in

43

little cocks. John wanted to lie on one of the hay-cocks with Lillian, but did not dare suggest it.

At the hotel John ate his dinner in silence. There wasn't even a traveling salesman in the dining-room, and presently the proprietor's wife came and stood by his table to talk with him. The hotel had a good many tourists, but this just happened to be a quiet day. Dull days came that way in the hotel business. The woman's husband was a traveling man and had bought the hotel to give his wife something to keep her interested while he was on the road. He was away from home so much! They had come to Caxton from Pittsburgh.

After he had dined, John went up to his room, and presently the woman followed. The door leading into the hall had been left open, and she came and stood in the doorway. Really, she was rather handsome. She only wanted to be sure that everything was all right, that he had towels and soap and everything he needed.

For a time she lingered by the door talking of the town.

"It's a good little town. General Hurst is buried here. You should drive out to the cemetery and see the statue." He wondered who General Hurst was. In what war had he fought. Odd that he hadn't remembered about him. The town had a piano factory, and there was a watch company from Cincinnati talking of putting up a plant. "They figure there is less chance of labor trouble in a small town like this."

The woman went reluctantly away. As she was going along the hallway she stopped once and looked back. There was something a little queer. They were both self-conscious. "I hope you'll be comfortable," she said. At forty a man did not come home to his own home town to start . . . A traveling man's wife, eh? Well! Well!

At seven forty-five John went out for a walk on Main Street and almost at once he met Tom Ballard, who at once recognized him, a fact that pleased Tom. He bragged about it. "Once I see a face, I never forget. Well! Well!" When John was twenty-two, Tom must have been about fifteen. His father was the leading doctor of the town. He took John in tow, walked back with him toward the hotel. He kept exclaiming: "I knew you at once. You haven't changed much, really."

Tom was in his turn a doctor, and there was about him something . . . Right away John guessed what it was. They went up into John's room, and John, having in his bag a bottle of whisky, poured Tom a drink, which he took somewhat too eagerly, John thought. There was talk. After Tom had taken

45

the drink he sat on the edge of the bed, still holding the bottle John had passed to him. Herman was running a dray now. He had married Kit Small and had five kids. Joe was working for the International Harvester Company. "I don't know whether he's in town now or not. He's a trouble-shooter, a swell mechanic, a good fellow," Tom said. He drank again.

As for Lillian, mentioned with an air of being casual by John, he, John, knew of course that she had been married and divorced. There was some sort of trouble about another man. Her husband married again later, and now she lived with her mother, her father, the shoe merchant, having died. Tom spoke somewhat guardedly, as though protecting a friend.

"I guess she's all right now, going straight and all. Good thing she never had any kids. She's a little nervous and queer; has lost her looks a good deal."

The two men went downstairs and, walking along Main Street, got into a car belonging to the doctor.

"I'll take you for a little ride," Tom said; but as he was about to pull away from the curb where the car had been parked, he turned and smiled at his passenger. "We ought to celebrate a little, account of your coming back here," he said. "What do you say to a quart?"

John handed him a ten-dollar bill, and he disappeared into a nearby drug store. When he came back he laughed.

"I used your name, all right. They didn't recognize it. In the prescription I wrote out I said you had a general breakdown, that you needed to be built up. I recommended that you take a teaspoonful three times a day. Lord! my prescription book is getting almost empty." The drug store belonged to a man named Will Bennett. "You remember him, maybe. He's Ed Bennett's son; married Carrie Wyatt." The names were but dim things in John's mind. "This man is going to get drunk. He is going to try to get me drunk, too," he thought.

When they had turned out of Main Street and into Walnut Street they stopped midway between two street lights and had another drink, John holding the bottle to his lips, but putting his tongue over the opening. He remembered the evenings with Joe and Herman when he had secretly poured his beer into a spittoon. He felt cold and lonely. Walnut Street was one along which he used to walk, coming home late at night from Lillian's house. He remembered people who then lived along the street, and a list of names began running through his head. Often the names remained, but did not call up images of people. They were just names. He hoped the doctor would not turn the car into the street in which the Holdens had lived. Lillian had lived over in another part of town, in what was called "The Red House District." Just why it had been called that John did not know.

III

THEY drove silently along, up a small hill, and came to the edge of town, going south. Stopping before a house that had evidently been built since John's time, Tom sounded his horn.

"Didn't the fair grounds used to stand about here?" John asked. The doctor turned and nodded his head.

"Yes, just here," he said. He kept on sounding his horn, and a man and woman came out of the house and stood in the road beside the car.

"Let's get Maud and Alf and all go over to Lylse's Point," Tom said. John had indeed been taken into tow. For a time he wondered if he was to be introduced. "We got some hooch. Meet John Holden; used to live here years ago." At the fair grounds, when John was a lad, Dave Grey, the livery man, used to work out his race horses in the early morning. Herman, who was a horse enthusiast, dreaming of some day becoming a horseman, came often to John's house in the early morning and the

48

two boys went off to the fair grounds without breakfast. Herman had got some sandwiches made of
slices of bread and cold meat out of his mother's
pantry. They went 'cross-lots, climbing fences and
eating the sandwiches. In a meadow they had to cross
there was heavy dew on the grass, and meadow larks
flew up before them. Herman had at least come
somewhere near expressing in his life his youthful
passion: he still lived about horses; he owned a dray.
With a little inward qualm John wondered. Perhaps Herman ran a motor-truck.

The man and woman got into the car, the
woman on the back seat with John, the husband in
front with Tom, and they drove away to another
house. John could not keep track of the streets they
passed through. Occasionally he asked the woman,
"What street are we in now?" They were joined by
Maud and Alf, who also crowded into the back seat.
Maud was a slender woman of twenty-eight or thirty,
with yellow hair and blue eyes, and at once she
seemed determined to make up to John. "I don't
take more than an inch of room," she said, laughing
and squeezing herself in between John and the first
woman, whose name he could not later remember.

He had rather liked Maud. When the car had
been driven some eighteen miles along a gravel road,
they came to Lylse's farmhouse, which had been con-

verted into a road-house, and got out. Maud had been silent most of the way, but she sat very close to John and as he felt cold and lonely, he was grateful for the warmth of her slender body. Occasionally she spoke to him in a half-whisper: "Ain't the night swell! Gee! I like it out in the dark this way."

Lylse's Point was at a bend of the Samson River, a small stream to which John as a lad had occasionally gone on fishing excursions with his father. Later he went out there several times with crowds of young fellows and their girls. They drove out then in Grey's old bus, and the trip out and back took several hours. On the way home at night they had great fun singing at the top of their voices and waking the sleeping farmers along the road. Occasionally some of the party got out and walked for a way. It was a chance for a fellow to kiss his girl when the others could not see. By hurrying a little, they could easily enough catch up with the bus.

A rather heavy-faced Italian named Francisco owned Lylse's, and it had a dance hall and dining-room. Drinks could be had if you knew the ropes, and it was evident the doctor and his friends were old acquaintances. At once they declared John should not buy anything, the declaration, in fact, being made before he had offered. "You're our guest now; don't you forget that. When we come sometime to your town, then it will be all right," Tom said. He laughed. "And that makes me think. I forgot your change," he said, handing John a five-dollar bill. The whisky got at the drug-store had been consumed on the way out, all except John and Maud drinking heartily. "I don't like the stuff. Do you, Mr. Holden?" Maud said and giggled. Twice during the trip out her fingers had crept over and touched lightly his fingers, and each time she had apologized. "Oh, do excuse me!" she said. John felt a little as he had felt earlier in the evening when the woman of the hotel had come to stand at the door of his room and had seemed reluctant about going away.

After they got out of the car at Lylse's, he felt uncomfortably old and queer. "What am I doing here with these people?" he kept asking himself. When they had got into the light, he stole a look at his watch. It was not yet nine o'clock. Several other cars, most of them, the doctor explained, from Yerington, stood before the door, and when they had taken several drinks of rather mild Italian red wine, all of the party except Maud and John went into the dance hall to dance. The doctor took John aside and whispered to him: "Lay off Maud," he said. He explained hurriedly that Alf and Maud had been having a row and that for several days they had not spoken to each other, although they lived in the same house, ate at the same table, and slept in the same bed. "He thinks she gets too gay with men," Tom explained. "You better look out a little."

The woman and man sat on a bench under a tree on the lawn before the house, and when the others had danced, they came out, bringing more drinks. Tom had got some more whisky. "It's moon, but pretty good stuff," he declared. In the clear sky overhead stars were shining, and when the others were dancing, John turned his head and saw across the road and between the trees that lined its banks the stars reflected in the waters of the Samson. A light from the house fell on Maud's face, a strikingly lovely face in that light, but when looked at closely, rather petulant. "A good deal of the spoiled child in her," John thought.

She began asking him about life in the city of New York.

"I was there once, but for only three days. It was when I went to school in the East. A girl I knew lived there. She married a lawyer named Trigan, or something like that. You didn't know him, I guess."

And now there was a hungry, dissatisfied look on her face.

"God! I'd like to live in a place like that, not in this hole! There hadn't no man better tempt me." When she said that she giggled again. Once during

the evening they walked across the dusty road and
stood for a time by the river's edge, but got back to
the bench before the others finished their dance.
Maud persistently refused to dance.

At ten thirty, all of the others having got a little
drunk, they drove back to town, Maud again sitting
beside John. On the drive Alf went to sleep. Maud
pressed her slender body against John's, and after
two or three futile moves to which he made no special response, she boldly put her hand into his. The
second woman and her husband talked with Tom of
people they had seen at Lylse's. "Do you think
there's anything up between Fanny and Joe? No;
I think she's on the square."

They got to John's hotel at eleven thirty, and,
bidding them all good night, he went upstairs. Alf
had awakened. When they were parting, he leaned
out of the car and looked closely at John. "What did
you say your name was?" he asked.

John went up a dark stairway and sat on the
bed in his room. Lillian had lost her looks. She had
married, and her husband had divorced her. Joe was
a trouble-shooter. He worked for the International
Harvester Company, a swell mechanic. Herman was
a drayman. He had five kids.

Three men in a room next to John's were playing poker. They laughed and talked, and their voices

came clearly to John. "You think so, do you? Well, I'll prove you're wrong." A mild quarrel began. As it was Summer, the windows of John's room were open, and he went to one to stand, looking out. A moon had come up, and he could see down into an alleyway. Two men came out of a street and stood in the alleyway, whispering. After they left, two cats crept along a roof and began a love-making scene. The game in the next room broke up. John could hear voices in the hallway.

"Now, forget it. I tell you, you're both wrong." John thought of his son at the camp up in Vermont. "I haven't written him a letter today." He felt guilty.

Opening his bag, he took out paper and sat down to write; but after two or three attempts gave it up and put the paper away again. How fine the night had been as he sat on the bench beside the woman at Lylse's! Now the woman was in bed with her husband. They were not speaking to each other.

"Could I do it?" John asked himself, and then, for the first time that evening, a smile came to his lips.

"Why not?" he asked himself.

With his bag in his hand he went down the dark hallway and into the hotel office and began pounding on a desk. A fat old man with thin red hair and sleep-heavy eyes appeared from somewhere. John explained.

"I can't sleep. I think I'll drive on. I want to get to Pittsburgh and as I can't sleep, I might as well be driving." He paid his bill.

Then he asked the clerk to go and arouse the man in the garage, and gave him an extra dollar. "If I need gas, is there any place open?" he asked, but evidently the man did not hear. Perhaps he thought the question absurd.

He stood in the moonlight on the sidewalk before the door of the hotel and heard the clerk pounding on a door. Presently voices were heard, and the headlights of his car shone. The car appeared, driven by a boy. He seemed very alive and alert.

"I saw you out to Lylse's," he said, and, without being asked, went to look at the tank. "You're all right; you got 'most eight gallons," he assured John, who had climbed into the driver's seat.

How friendly the car, how friendly the night! John was not one who enjoyed fast driving, but he went out of the town at very high speed. "You go down two blocks, turn to your right, and go three. There you hit the cement. Go right straight to the east. You can't miss it."

John was taking the turns at racing speed. At the edge of town some one shouted to him from the darkness, but he did not stop. He hungered to get into the road going east.

"I'll let her out," he thought. "Lord! It will be fun! I'll let her out."

THERE SHE IS—
SHE IS TAKING HER BATH

THERE SHE IS—
SHE IS TAKING HER BATH

ANOTHER day when I have done no work. It is maddening. I went to the office this morning as usual and tonight came home at the regular time. My wife and I live in an apartment in the Bronx, here in New York City, and we have no children. I am ten years older than she. Our apartment is on the second floor and there is a little hallway downstairs used by all the people in the building.

If I could only decide whether or not I am a fool, a man turned suddenly a little mad or a man whose honor has really been tampered with, I should be quite all right. Tonight I went home, after something most unusual had happened at the office, determined to tell everything to my wife. "I will tell her and then watch her face. If she blanches, then I will know all I suspect is true," I said to myself. Within the last two weeks everything about me has changed. I am no longer the same man. For example, I never in my life before used the word "blanched." What does it mean? How am I to tell whether my wife blanches or not when I do not know what the word means? It must be a word I saw in a book when I was a boy, perhaps a book of detective stories. But wait, I know how that happened to pop into my head.

But that is not what I started to tell you about. Tonight, as I have already said, I came home and climbed the stairs to our apartment.

When I got inside the house I spoke in a loud voice to my wife. "My dear, what are you doing?" I asked. My voice sounded strange.

"I am taking a bath," my wife answered.

And so you see she was at home taking a bath. There she was.

She is always pretending she loves me, but look at her now. Am I in her thoughts? Is there a tender look in her eyes? Is she dreaming of me as she walks along the streets?

You see she is smiling. There is a young man who has just passed her. He is a tall fellow with a little mustache and is smoking a cigarette. Now I ask you—is he one of the men who, like myself, does, in a way, keep the world going?

Once I knew a man who was president of a whist club. Well, he was something. People wanted to know how to play whist. They wrote to him. "If it turns out that after three cards are played the man to my right still has three cards while I have only two, etc., etc."

My friend, the man of whom I am now speaking, looks the matter up. "In rule four hundred and six you will see, etc., etc.," he writes.

My point is that he is of some account in the world. He helps keep things going and I respect him. Often we used to have lunch together.

But I am a little off the point. The fellows of whom I am now thinking, these young squirts who go through the streets ogling women—what do they do? They twirl their mustaches. They carry canes. Some honest man is supporting them too. Some fool is their father.

And such a fellow is walking in the street. He meets a woman like my wife, an honest woman without too much experience of life. He smiles. A tender look comes into his eyes. Such deceit. Such callow nonsense.

And how are the women to know? They are children. They know nothing. There is a man, working somewhere in an office, keeping things moving, but do they think of him?

The truth is the woman is flattered. A tender look, that should be saved and bestowed only upon her husband, is thrown away. One never knows what will happen.

But pshaw, if I am to tell you the story, let me begin. There are men everywhere who talk and talk, saying nothing. I am afraid I am becoming one of that kind. As I have already told you, I have come home from the office at evening and am standing in the hallway of our apartment, just inside the door. I have asked my wife what she is doing and she has told me she is taking a bath.

Very well, I am then a fool. I shall go out for a walk in the park. There is no use my not facing everything frankly. By facing everything frankly one gets everything quite cleared up.

Aha! The very devil has got into me now. I said I would remain cool and collected, but I am not cool. The truth is I am growing angry.

I am a small man but I tell you that, once aroused, I will fight. Once when I was a boy I fought another boy in the school yard. He gave me a black eye but I loosened one of his teeth. "There, take that and that. Now I have got you against a wall. I will muss your mustache. Give me that cane. I will break it over your head. I do not intend to kill you, young man. I intend to vindicate my honor. No, I will not let you go. Take that and that. When next you see a respectable married woman on the street, going to the store, behaving herself, do not look at her with a tender light in your eyes. What you

62

had better do is to go to work. Get a job in a bank. Work your way up. You said I was an old goat but I will show you an old goat can butt. Take that and that."

Very well, you, who read, also think me a fool. You laugh. You smile. Look at me. You are walking along here in the park. You are leading a dog.

Where is your wife? What is she doing?

Well, suppose she is at home taking a bath. What is she thinking? If she is dreaming, as she takes her bath, of whom is she dreaming?

I will tell you what, you who go along leading that dog, you may have no reason to suspect your wife, but you are in the same position as myself.

She was at home taking a bath and all day I had been sitting at my desk and thinking such thoughts. Under the circumstances I would never have had the temerity to go calmly off and take a bath. I admire my wife. Ha, ha. If she is innocent I admire her, of course, as a husband should, and if she is guilty I admire her even more. What nerve, what insouciance. There is something noble, something almost heroic in her attitude toward me, just at this time.

With me this day is like every day now. Well, you see, I have been sitting all day with my head in my hand thinking and thinking and while I have been doing that she has been going about, leading her regular life.

She has got up in the morning and has had her breakfast sitting opposite her husband; that is, myself. Her husband has gone off to his office. Now she is speaking to our maid. She is going to the stores. She is sewing, perhaps making new curtains for the windows of our apartment.

There is the woman for you. Nero fiddled while Rome was burning. There was something of the woman in him.

A wife has been unfaithful to her husband. She has gone gayly off, let us say on the arm of a young blade. Who is he? He dances. He smokes cigarettes. When he is with his companions, his own kind of fellows, he laughs. "I have got me a woman," he says. "She is not very young but she is terrifically in love with me. It is very convenient." I have heard such fellows talk, in the smoking cars, on trains and in other places.

And there is the husband, a fellow like myself. Is he calm? Is he collected? Is he cool? His honor is perhaps being tampered with. He sits at his desk. He smokes a cigar. People come and go. He is thinking, thinking.

And what are his thoughts? They concern her. "Now she is still at home, in our apartment," he thinks. "Now she is walking along a street." What do you know of the secret life led by your wife? What do you know of her thoughts? Well, hello! You smoke a pipe. You put your hands in your pockets. For you, your life is all very well. You are gay and happy. "What does it matter, my wife is at home taking a bath," you are telling yourself. In your daily life you are, let us say, a useful man. You publish books, you run a store, you write advertisements. Sometimes you say to yourself, "I am lifting the burden off the shoulders of others." That makes you feel good. I sympathize with you. If you let me, or rather I should say, if we had met in the formal transactions of our regular occupations, I dare say we would be great friends. Well, we would have lunch together, not too often, but now and then. I would tell you of some real-estate deal and you would tell me what you had been doing. "I am glad we met! Call me up. Before you go away, have a cigar."

With me it is quite different. All today, for example, I have been in my office, but I have not worked. A man came in, a Mr. Albright. "Well, are you going to let that property go or are you going to hold on?" he said.

What property did he mean? What was he talking about?

65

You can see for yourself what a state I am in.

And now I must be going home. My wife will have finished taking her bath. We will sit down to dinner. Nothing of all this I have been speaking about will be mentioned at all. "John, what is the matter with you?" "Aha. There is nothing the matter. I am worried about business a little. A Mr. Albright came in. Shall I sell or shall I hold on?" The real thing that is on my mind shall not be mentioned at all. I will grow a little nervous. The coffee will be spilled on the table-cloth or I will upset my dessert.

"John, what is the matter with you?" What coolness. As I have already said, what insouciance.

What is the matter? Matter enough.

A week, two weeks, to be exact, just seventeen days ago, I was a happy man. I went about my affairs. In the morning I rode to my office in the subway, but, had I wished to do so, I could long ago have bought an automobile.

But no, long ago, my wife and I had agreed there should be no such silly extravagance. To tell the truth, just ten years ago I failed in business and had to put some property in my wife's name. I bring the papers home to her and she signs. That is the way it is done.

"Well, John," said my wife, "we will not get us any automobile." That was before the thing happened that so upset me. We were walking together in the park. "Mabel, shall we get us an automobile?" I asked. "No," she said, "we will not get us an automobile." "Our money," she has said, more than a thousand times, "will be a comfort to us later."

A comfort indeed. What can be a comfort now that this thing has happened?

It was just two weeks, more than that, just seventeen days ago, that I went home from the office just as I came home tonight. Well, I walked in the same streets, passed the same stores.

I am puzzled as to what that Mr. Albright meant when he asked me if I intended to sell the property or hold on to it. I answered in a noncommittal way. "We'll see," I said. To what property did he refer? We must have had some previous conversation regarding the matter. A mere acquaintance does not come into your office and speak of property in that careless, one might say, familiar way, without having previous conversation on the same subject.

As you see I am still a little confused. Even though I am facing things now, I am still, as you have guessed, somewhat confused. This morning I was in the bathroom, shaving as usual. I always shave in the morning, not in the evening, unless my wife and I are going out. I was shaving and my shaving brush dropped to the floor. I stooped to pick it up and struck my head on the bath-tub. I only tell you this to show what a state I am in. It made a large bump on my head. My wife heard me groan and asked me what was the matter. "I struck my head," I said. Of course, one quite in control of his faculties does not hit his head on a bath-tub when he knows it is there, and what man does not know where the bath-tub stands in his own house?

But now I am thinking again of what happened, of what has upset me this way. I was going home on that evening, just seventeen days ago. Well, I walked along, thinking nothing. When I reached our apartment building I went in, and there, lying on the floor in the little hallway, in front, was a pink envelope with my wife's name, Mabel Smith, written on it. I picked it up thinking, "This is strange." It had perfume on it and there was no address, just the name Mabel Smith, written in a bold man's hand.

I quite automatically opened it and read.

Since I first met her, twelve years ago at a party at Mr. Westley's house, there have never been any secrets between me and my wife; at least, until that moment in the hallway seventeen days ago this evening, I had never thought there were any secrets between us. I have always opened her letters and she had always opened mine. I think it should be

that way between a man and his wife. I know there
are some who do not agree with me but what I have
always argued is I am right.

I went to the party with Harry Selfridge and
afterward took my wife home. I offered to get a cab.
"Shall we have a cab?" I asked her. "No," she said,
"let's walk." She was the daughter of a man in the
furniture business and he has died since. Every one
thought he would leave her some money but he
didn't. It turned out he owed almost all he was
worth to a firm in Grand Rapids. Some would have
been upset, but I wasn't. "I married you for love,
my dear," I said to her on the night when her father
died. We were walking home from his house, also
in the Bronx, and it was raining a little, but we did
not get very wet. "I married you for love," I said,
and I meant what I said.

But to return to the note. "Dear Mabel," it
said, "come to the park on Wednesday when the old
goat has gone away. Wait for me on the bench near
the animal cages where I met you before."

It was signed Bill. I put it in my pocket and
went upstairs.

When I got into my apartment, I heard a man's
voice. The voice was urging something upon my
wife. Did the voice change when I came in? I walked
boldly into our front room where my wife sat facing

a young man who sat in another chair. He was tall and had a little mustache.

The man was pretending to be trying to sell my wife a patent carpet-sweeper, but just the same, when I sat down in a chair in the corner and remained there, keeping silent, they both became self-conscious. My wife, in fact, became positively excited. She got up out of her chair and said in a loud voice, "I tell you I do not want any carpet-sweeper."

The young man got up and went to the door and I followed. "Well, I had better be getting out of here," he was saying to himself. And so he had been intending to leave a note telling my wife to meet him in the park on Wednesday but at the last moment he had decided to take the risk of coming to our house. What he had probably thought was something like this: "Her husband may come and get the note out of the mail box." Then he decided to come and see her and had quite accidentally dropped the note in the hallway. Now he was frightened. One could see that. Such men as myself are small but we will fight sometimes.

He hurried to the door and I followed him into the hallway. There was another young man coming from the floor above, also with a carpet-sweeper in his hand. It is a pretty slick scheme, this carrying carpet-sweepers with them, the young men of this generation have worked out, but we older men are not to have the wool pulled over our eyes. I saw through everything at once. The second young man was a confederate and had been concealed in the hallway in order to warn the first young man of my approach. When I got upstairs, of course, the first young man was pretending to sell my wife a carpet-sweeper. Perhaps the second young man had tapped with the handle of the carpet-sweeper on the floor above. Now that I think of that I remember there was a tapping sound.

At the time, however, I did not think everything out as I have since done. I stood in the hallway with my back against the wall and watched them go down the stairs. One of them turned and laughed at me, but I did not say anything. I suppose I might have gone down the stairs after them and challenged them both to fight but what I thought was, "I won't."

And sure enough, just as I suspected from the first, it was the young man pretending to sell carpet-sweepers I had found sitting in my apartment with my wife, who had lost the note. When they got down to the hallway at the front of the house the man I had caught with my wife began to feel in his pocket. Then, as I leaned over the railing above,

71

I saw him looking about the hallway. He laughed. "Say, Tom, I had a note to Mabel in my pocket. I intended to get a stamp at the postoffice and mail it. I had forgotten the street number. 'Oh, well,' I thought, 'I'll go see her!' I didn't want to bump into that old goat, her husband."

"You have bumped into him," I said to myself; "now we will see who will come out victorious."

I went into our apartment and closed the door.

For a long time, perhaps for ten minutes, I stood just inside the door of our apartment thinking and thinking, just as I have been doing ever since. Two or three times I tried to speak, to call out to my wife, to question her and find out the bitter truth at once but my voice failed me.

What was I to do? Was I to go to her, seize her by the wrists, force her down into a chair, make her confess at the risk of personal violence? I asked myself that question.

"No," I said to myself, "I will not do that. I will use finesse."

For a long time I stood there thinking. My world had tumbled down about my ears. When I tried to speak, the words would not come out of my mouth.

At last I did speak, quite calmly. There is something of the man of the world about me. When I am compelled to meet a situation I do it. "What are you doing?" I said to my wife, speaking in a calm voice. "I am taking a bath," she answered.

And so I left the house and came out here to the park to think, just as I have done tonight. On that night, and just as I came out at our front door, I did something I have not done since I was a boy. I am a deeply religious man but I swore. My wife and I have had a good many arguments as to whether or not a man in business should have dealings with those who do such things; that is to say, with men who swear. "I cannot refuse to sell a man a piece of property because he swears," I have always said. "Yes, you can," my wife says.

It only shows how little women know about business. What I have always maintained is I am right.

And I maintain too that we men must protect the integrity of our homes and our firesides. On that first night I walked about until dinner time and then went home. I had decided not to say anything for the present but to remain quiet and use finesse, but at dinner my hand trembled and I spilled the dessert on the table-cloth.

And a week later I went to see a detective.

But first something else happened. On Wednesday—I had found the note on Monday evening—I

could not bear sitting in my office and thinking perhaps that that young squirt was meeting my wife
in the park, so I went to the park myself.

Sure enough there was my wife sitting on a
bench near the animal cages and knitting a sweater.

At first I thought I would conceal myself in
some bushes but instead I went to where she was
seated and sat down beside her. "How nice! What
brings you here?" my wife said smiling. She looked
at me with surprise in her eyes.

Was I to tell her or was I not to tell her? It
was a moot question with me. "No," I said to myself.
"I will not. I will go see a detective. My honor has
no doubt already been tampered with and I shall
find out." My naturally quick wits came to my res-
cue. Looking directly into my wife's eyes I said:
"There was a paper to be signed and I had my
own reasons for thinking you might be here, in the
park."

As soon as I had spoken I could have torn out
my tongue. However, she had noticed nothing and
I took a paper out of my pocket and, handing her
my fountain pen, asked her to sign; and when she
had done so I hurried away. At first I thought perhaps I would linger about, in the distance, that is
to say, but no, I decided not to do that. He will

no doubt have his confederate on the watchout for me, I told myself.

And so on the next afternoon, I went to the office of the detective. He was a large man, and when I told him what I wanted he smiled. "I understand," he said, "we have many such cases. We'll track the guy down."

And so, you see, there it was. Everything was arranged. It was to cost me a pretty penny but my house was to be watched and I was to have a report on everything. To tell the truth, when everything was arranged I felt ashamed of myself. The man in the detective place—there were several men standing about—followed me to the door and put his hand on my shoulder. For some reason I don't understand, that made me mad. He kept patting me on the shoulder as though I were a little boy. "Don't worry. We'll manage everything," was what he said. It was all right. Business is business but for some reason I wanted to bang him in the face with my fist.

That's the way I am, you see. I can't make myself out. "Am I a fool, or am I a man among men?" I keep asking myself, and I can't get an answer.

After I had arranged with the detective I went home and didn't sleep all night long.

To tell the truth I began to wish I had never

found that note. I suppose that is wrong of me. It makes me less a man, perhaps, but it's the truth.

Well, you see, I couldn't sleep. "No matter what my wife was up to I could sleep now if I hadn't found that note," was what I said to myself. It was dreadful. I was ashamed of what I had done and at the same time ashamed of myself for being ashamed. I had done what any American man, who is a man at all, would have done, and there I was. I couldn't sleep. Every time I came home in the evening I kept thinking: "There is that man standing over there by a tree—I'll bet he is a detective." I kept thinking of the fellow who had patted me on the shoulders in the detective office, and every time I thought of him I grew madder and madder. Pretty soon I hated him more than I did the young man who had pretended to sell the carpet-sweeper to Mabel.

And then I did the most foolish thing of all. One afternoon—it was just a week ago—I thought of something. When I had been in the detective office I had seen several men standing about but had not been introduced to any of them. "And so," I thought, "I'll go there pretending to get my reports. If the man I engaged is not there I'll engage some one else."

So I did it. I went to the detective office, and

sure enough my man was out. There was another fellow sitting by a desk and I made a sign to him. We went into an inner office. "Look here," I whispered; you see I had made up my mind to pretend I was the man who was ruining my own fireside, wrecking my own honor. "Do I make clear what I mean?"

It was like this, you see—well, I had to have some sleep, didn't I? Only the night before my wife had said to me, "John, I think you had better run away for a little vacation. Run away by yourself for a time and forget about business."

At another time her saying that would have been nice, you see, but now it only upset me worse than ever. "She wants me out of the way," I thought, and for just a moment I felt like jumping up and telling her everything I knew. Still I didn't. "I'll just keep quiet. I'll use finesse," I thought.

A pretty kind of finesse. There I was in that detective office again hiring a second detective. I came right out and pretended I was my wife's paramour. The man kept nodding his head and I kept whispering like a fool. Well, I told him that a man named Smith had hired a detective from that office to watch his wife. "I have my own reasons for wanting him to get a report that his wife is all right," I said, pushing some money across a table toward

77

him. I had become utterly reckless about money. "Here is fifty dollars and when he gets such a report from your office you come to me and you may have two hundred more," I said.

I had thought everything out. I told the second man my name was Jones and that I worked in the same office with Smith. "I'm in business with him," I said, "a silent partner, you see."

Then I went out and, of course, he, like the first one, followed me to the door and patted me on the shoulder. That was the hardest thing of all to stand, but I stood it. A man has to have sleep.

And, of course, today both men had to come to my office within five minutes of each other. The first one came, of course, and told me my wife was innocent. "She is as innocent as a little lamb," he said. "I congratulate you upon having such an innocent wife."

Then I paid him, backing away so he couldn't pat me on the shoulders, and he had only just closed the door when in came the other man, asking for Jones.

And I had to see him too and give him two hundred dollars.

Then I decided to come on home, and I did, walking along the same street I have walked on every afternoon since my wife and I married. I went

home and climbed the stairs to our apartment just
as I described everything to you a little while ago.
I could not decide whether I was a fool, a man who
has gone a little mad, or a man whose honor has
been tampered with, but anyway I knew there would
be no detectives about.

What I thought was that I would go home and
have everything out with my wife, tell her of my
suspicions and then watch her face. As I have said
before, I intended to watch her face and see if she
blanched when I told her of the note I had found
in the hallway downstairs. The word "blanched"
got into my mind because I once read it in a detective story when I was a boy and I had been dealing
with detectives.

And so I intended to face my wife down, force
a confession from her, but you see how it turned out.
When I got home the apartment was silent and at
first I thought it was empty. "Has she run away
with him?" I asked myself, and maybe my own face
blanched a little.

"Where are you, dear, what are you doing?"
I shouted in a loud voice and she told me she was
taking a bath.

And so I came out here in the park.

But now I must be going home. Dinner will
be waiting. I am wondering what property that Mr.

Albright had in his mind. When I sit at dinner with my wife my hands will shake. I will spill the dessert. A man does not come in and speak of property in that offhand manner unless there has been conversation about it before.

THE LOST NOVEL

THE LOST NOVEL

H E said it was all like a dream. A man like that, a writer. Well, he works for months and, perhaps, years, on a book, and there is not a word put down. What I mean is that his mind is working. What is to be the book builds itself up and is destroyed.

In his fancy, figures are moving back and forth.

But there is something I neglected to say. I am talking of a certain English novelist who has got some fame, of a thing that once happened to him.

He told me about it one day in London when we were walking together. We had been together for hours. I remember that we were on the Thames Embankment when he told me about his lost novel.

He had come to see me early in the evening at my hotel. He spoke of certain stories of my own. "You almost get at something, sometimes," he said.

We agreed that no man ever quite got at—the thing.

If some one once got at it, if he really put the ball over the plate, you know, if he hit the bull's-eye.

What would be the sense of anyone trying to do anything after that?

I'll tell you what, some of the old fellows have come pretty near.

Keats, eh? And Shakespeare. And George Borrow and DeFoe.

We spent a half hour going over names.

We went off to dine together and later walked. He was a little, black, nervous man with ragged locks of hair sticking out from under his hat.

I began talking of his first book.

But here is a brief outline of his history. He came from a poor farming family in some English village. He was like all writers. From the very beginning he wanted to write.

He had no education. At twenty he got married.

She must have been a very respectable, nice girl. If I remember rightly she was the daughter of a priest of the Established English Church.

Just the kind he should not have married. But who shall say whom anyone shall love—or marry? She was above him in station. She had been to a woman's college; she was well educated.

I have no doubt she thought him an ignorant man.

"She thought me a sweet man, too. The hell

84

with that," he said, speaking of it. "I am not sweet. I hate sweetness."

We had got to that sort of intimacy, walking in the London night, going now and then into a pub to get a drink.

I remember that we each got a bottle, fearing the pubs would close before we got through talking.

What I told him about myself and my own adventures I can't remember.

The point is he wanted to make some kind of a pagan out of his woman, and the possibilities weren't in her.

They had two kids.

Then suddenly he did begin to burst out writing—that is to say, really writing.

You know a man like that. When he writes he writes. He had some kind of a job in his English town. I believe he was a clerk.

Because he was writing, he, of course, neglected his job, his wife, his kids.

He used to walk about the fields at night. His wife scolded. Of course, she was all broken up—would be. No woman can quite bear the absolute way in which a man who has been her lover can sometimes drop her when he is at work.

I mean an artist, of course. They can be first-class lovers. It may be they are the only lovers.

And they are absolutely ruthless about throwing direct personal love aside.

You can imagine that household. The man told me there was a little bedroom upstairs in the house where they were living at that time. This was while he was still in the English town.

The man used to come home from his job and go upstairs. Upstairs he went and locked his door. Often he did not stop to eat, and sometimes he did not even speak to his wife.

He wrote and wrote and wrote and threw away.

Then he lost his job. "The hell," he said, when he spoke of it.

He didn't care, of course. What is a job?

What is a wife or child? There must be a few ruthless people in this world.

Pretty soon there was practically no food in the house.

He was upstairs in that room behind the door, writing. The house was small and the children cried. "The little brats," he said, speaking of them. He did not mean that, of course. I understand what he meant. His wife used to come and sit on the stairs outside the door, back of which he was at work. She cried audibly and the child she had in her arms cried.

"A patient soul, eh?" the English novelist said

86

to me when he told me of it. "And a good soul, too," he said. "To hell with her," he also said.

You see, he had begun writing about her. She was what his novel was about, his first one. In time it may prove to be his best one.

Such tenderness of understanding—of her difficulties and her limitations, and such a casual, brutal way of treating her, personally.

Well, if we have a soul, that is worth something, eh?

It got so they were never together a moment without quarreling.

And then one night he struck her. He had forgotten to fasten the door of the room in which he worked. She came bursting in.

And just as he was getting at something about her, some understanding of the reality of her. Any writer will understand the difficulty of his position. In a fury he rushed at her, struck her and knocked her down.

And then, well, she quit him then. Why not? However, he finished the book. It was a real book.

But about his lost novel. He said he came up to London after his wife left him and began living alone. He thought he would write another novel.

You understand that he had got recognition, had been acclaimed.

And the second novel was just as difficult to write as the first. It may be that he was a good deal exhausted.

And, of course, he was ashamed. He was ashamed of the way in which he had treated his wife. He tried to write another novel so that he wouldn't always be thinking. He told me that, for the next year or two, the words he wrote on the paper were all wooden. Nothing was alive.

Months and months of that sort of thing. He withdrew from people. Well, what about his children? He sent money to his wife and went to see her once.

He said she was living with her father's people, and he went to her father's house and got her. They went to walk in the fields. "We couldn't talk," he said. "She began to cry and called me a crazy man. Then I glared at her, as I had once done that time I struck her, and she turned and ran away from me back to her father's house, and I came away."

Having written one splendid novel, he wanted, of course, to write some more. He said there were all sorts of characters and situations in his head. He used to sit at his desk for hours writing and then go out in the streets and walk as he and I walked together that night.

Nothing would come right for him.

He had got some sort of theory about himself. He said that the second novel was inside him like an unborn child. His conscience was hurting him about his wife and children. He said he loved them all right but did not want to see them again.

Sometimes he thought he hated them. One evening, he said, after he had been struggling like that, and long after he had quit seeing people, he wrote his second novel. It happened like this.

All morning he had been sitting in his room. It was a small room he had rented in a poor part of London. He had got out of bed early, and without eating any breakfast had begun to write. And everything he wrote that morning was also no good.

About three o'clock in the afternoon, as he had been in the habit of doing, he went out to walk. He took a lot of writing-paper with him.

"I had an idea I might begin to write at any time," he said.

He went walking in Hyde Park. He said it was a clear, bright day, and people were walking about together. He sat on a bench.

He hadn't eaten anything since the night before. As he sat there he tried a trick. Later I heard that a group of young poets in Paris took up that sort of thing and were profoundly serious about it.

The Englishman tried what is called "automatic writing."

He just put his pencil on the paper and let the pencil make what words it would.

Of course the pencil made a queer jumble of absurd words. He quit doing that.

There he sat on the bench staring at the people walking past.

He was tired, like a man who has been in love for a long time with some woman he cannot get.

Let us say there are difficulties. He is married or she is. They look at each other with promises in their eyes and nothing happens.

Wait and wait. Most people's lives are spent waiting.

And then suddenly, he said, he began writing his novel. The theme, of course, was men and women —lovers. What other theme is there for such a man? He told me that he must have been thinking a great deal of his wife and of his cruelty to her. He wrote and wrote. The evening passed and night came. Fortunately, there was a moon. He kept on writing. He said it was the most intense writing he ever did or ever hoped to do. Hours and hours passed. He sat there on that bench writing like a crazy man.

He wrote a novel at one sitting. Then he went home to his room.

He said he never was so happy and satisfied with himself in his life.

"I thought that I had done justice to my wife and to my children, to everyone and everything," he said. If they did not know it, never would know— what difference would that make?

He said that all the love he had in his being went into the novel.

He took it home and laid it on his desk.

What a sweet feeling of satisfaction to have done —the thing.

Then he went out of his room and found an all-night place where he could get something to eat.

After he got food he walked around the town. How long he walked he didn't know.

Then he went home and slept. It was daylight by this time. He slept all through the next day.

He said that when he woke up he thought he would look at his novel. "I really knew all the time it wasn't there," he said. "On the desk, of course, there was nothing but blank empty sheets of paper.

"Anyway," he said, "this I know. I never will write such a beautiful novel as that one was."

When he said it he laughed.

I do not believe there are too many people in

the world who will know exactly what he was laughing about.

But why be so arbitrary? There may be even a dozen.

THE FIGHT

THE FIGHT

T H E man—the guest—came up out of the garden
to the porch of the house. He had a flat even voice.
He was rather bulky. Immediately he began to talk.

The man of the house—his name was John
Wilder—had to make a special effort to seem atten-
tive. "Now I shall have to listen to some more of
his gabble. He is trying to be polite."

What the guest had to say amounted to nothing.
He spoke of the sunset. The porch of the house faced
the west. Yes, yes, there was a sunset. There was a
gray stone wall at the end of the garden and, beyond,
a hill. On the side of the hill were a few apple trees.

The guest was also named Wilder—Alfred
Wilder. He was John Wilder's cousin.

They were both substantial-looking men. John
Wilder was a lawyer, his cousin a scientist who did
some sort of experimental work for a large manu-
facturing company in another city.

The two cousins had not seen each other for
several years. Alfred Wilder's wife was in Europe

with his daughter. They were spending the Summer over there.

For years there had been no correspondence between the two men. They were both born in the same Middle-Western American small town. When they were boys they lived on the same street.

There had always been something wrong with their relationship. When they were small boys they always wanted to fight.

They never did. There were other children in both families. The cousins always played together. At Christmas time they gave each other presents. It was presumed they had for each other a cousinly feeling. Some one was always presuming that. The fools!

There was a combined Christmas celebration held by the two families. John had to buy a present for Alfred and Alfred had to buy one for John.

That day at John Wilder's house, when both men were nearly fifty years old and when Alfred was speaking of the sunset, John was thinking of a Christmas of his youth.

There had been another boy on the street who had a dog with several small puppies. The boy—a special friend—had given one to John. He had been delighted and had taken it home.

But his mother did not like dogs. She would

not let him keep it. He stood in tears holding the puppy in his arms. He had been commanded to take it back where he got it, but at the last moment he had an idea.

John's mother knew his cousin Alfred wanted a dog. John would keep it for a time but give it to his cousin as a Christmas present. It was such a sweet idea. It had just popped into his head. He had never intended to do it.

He would keep the puppy around. His mother would grow fond of it. When he said he would give it to his cousin he was being like the master of a vessel in a storm. He was putting into the nearest port, taking certain chances to save a vessel—or a pup.

He had got the pup in the late Fall. He kept it in the barn back of the house.

He went to see it twenty times a day. At night sometimes he crept out of bed and went to visit the pup.

His mother paid no attention. The pup had made no progress with her. John had another idea. He would so win the affection of the pup that when he gave it to his cousin and his cousin took it home, it would not stay.

The pup would keep on coming back and back. In the end his mother would surrender.

John had heard many stories about the affection of dogs. You win the affection of a dog once and he will never desert you. If you die he will come and howl over your grave.

John had felt like dying when he thought of Alfred owning the pup. He had wanted to die.

If he were dead it would pay his mother out—well, a dead boy buried in the snow. Snow on his grave, a dead pup lying across the grave. It had died of grief. Tears came into John's eyes when he thought of the scene.

As has been suggested John had got the puppy in the Fall. At Christmas time he had to give it to his cousin and Alfred had given him a cheap watch with a chain. It wasn't really his gift. His father had to put up the money.

Alfred took the pup home and John waited. It did not come back. He began to hate the pup.

He decided that Alfred had locked it up and went to see. When he got to his cousin's house his cousin wasn't at home. He had gone skating.

However, the pup was in the yard. John called but the pup would not come. He just stood wagging his tail. Then he barked as though John were some stranger.

John went away hating the dog. His hatred of

his cousin had always been an unreasonable thing in him and he was often ashamed of it.

The pup grew into doghood. It was a shepherd dog.

One day John was in a field near the town. He was sixteen then. He had a gun, his father's gun, and was out hunting rabbits.

He was in a small wood and suddenly, in a nearby field, he saw the dog. He was a big shaggy fellow now, an ugly-looking dog, John thought. There were sheep in the field. The dog was creeping along a fence toward the sheep.

John had heard of sheep-killing dogs. Just at that time there had been several sheep killed one night in a field near the town.

John went along the fence toward the dog. Of course the dog knew him. He was called "Shep." When he saw John he began wagging his tail.

Undoubtedly there was a guilty look in the dog's face. John became stern. It is every good citizen's duty to kill at sight a sheep-killing dog. John had never thought of the obligation involved in citizenship until that moment. Suddenly he became filled with it. He shot the dog. He had to fire both barrels of a double-barreled gun. The first shot crippled the dog and he howled with pain, but the second shot finished him off.

It was an oddly satisfactory feeling to see him die. John was ashamed of the feeling.

He was ashamed and at the same time glad. How pleasant that he had the excuse of thinking the dog was about to attack the sheep. Of course he could not be quite sure. No one knew he had killed the dog. He told no one. It was discovered later lying dead in the field. There were sheep pastured in the field. . . . Well, Alfred had become attached to the dog and was all broken up.

It wasn't however because Alfred was particularly affectionate—John knew that. He was just rubbing it in.

He was fond of the dog because he knew in his heart John had not wanted to give it to him. He was that kind.

John wasn't like that. He remembered Alfred's present. It was really his uncle's present. John had lost the watch right away. It slipped out of his pocket. The chain wasn't fastened. Well, it was a cheap watch.

He might have kept the watch and taken it out of his pocket from time to time when Alfred was about. Neither boy wanted to give the other a present. They had to. Their parents made them.

Taking the watch out of his pocket in that way would have plagued Alfred.

John had felt that, in losing the watch, he had been in some obscure way generous. However, he never boasted of his generosity.

He just knew that Alfred wasn't generous. After John had given him the pup at Christmas, it got sick. It might have died but that Alfred took extra good care of it. He even took it to a veterinary. "It just shows how some people are," John said to himself.

The two boys had grown up in a small town never having a fight. They left the town and went to different colleges. When they struck out into life they went to different cities.

Their hatred of each other continued. When they grew older and had to communicate with each other—for family reasons—they were always elaborately polite.

When John advanced a little in life—for example, when he served a term in Congress—Alfred wrote to congratulate him. John did the same thing when something good happened to Alfred. Both men got married, but in each case the other found it impossible to go to the wedding.

It happened that both men were a little ill just at that time. It was a coincidence. John was always glad it happened to him first. He used to tell himself that, had he married first and had Alfred been

ill, when it came Alfred's time to marry he would
have been there if he had had to get up out of his
death bed.

"I would never have let him know how ill I
was. Or, at least I would have thought up some other
excuse."

That was just the trouble. Neither man had
ever let the other know how he felt.

When they grew older it was more difficult.
For years they never corresponded.

And then Alfred came to visit John. John's
house was in a suburb in Chicago and Alfred had
some business in the city.

He had merely intended coming to John's
house for a casual call but John had urged him to
stay.

The more he hated Alfred the more he kept
urging him. That was because he felt guilty. He
hated himself for being such a fool.

It had happened also that John's wife had taken
a liking to his cousin Alfred. Sometimes the two sat
together for hours. They were both interested in
music. John wasn't. His wife played the piano.
Sometimes she played for Alfred all evening. She
played a while and then she and Alfred talked.
When Alfred's wife came back from Europe, John's

wife said, they would both have to come for a long visit. They would have to bring their daughter.

John and his wife had no children.

When he heard his vife ask the whole family to visit his house, John cringed. He was quite sure Alfred's daughter must be a fast, vulgar girl.

John sat in a chair reading a book and Alfred was with his wife in another room. John doubled his fists. His hatred of Alfred amused him sometimes. There was no reason for it. "It's just silly," he told himself.

On the evening when the two men were alone together on the porch of the house, John's wife was not at home. They had dined an hour earlier. Alfred's visit was almost over. He was leaving in two or three days.

He had said something about the beauty of the sunset and John had nodded his head.

Then both grew silent. The silence lasted a long time. It got rather heavy.

"Let's go for a walk," Alfred said.

John did not want to go. He did not know what else to do. His wife had gone to some kind of a women's club meeting. She would be gone all evening. He hated women's clubs.

John's house stood on a bluff that led down to

a lake. Beyond a garden wall there was a stairway going down to the beach.

The two men climbed down. It was a Summer night and some young men and women were in bathing.

John and Alfred did not speak to each other going down, and on the beach the silence between them continued. Minutes seemed to become hours.

Well, it wasn't unbearable. Both men were standing it.

It was all they could stand. They walked a little way along the beach and sat on the sand.

Time passed. Each man was telling himself the same thing. "I am utterly foolish. Here is my cousin. He is all right. What is the matter with him? I had better say, 'What is the matter with me.'"

They really wanted to fight. It was an absurd idea. They should have done it when they were boys. They were men of fifty, respectable men. Presently the young people on the beach went away. They were alone together.

John got to his feet and Alfred also started to rise. The sand may have been somewhat slippery. He fell against John.

John pushed him violently, sent him sprawling. He had not intended to. He just did it. His hand wouldn't behave.

THE FIGHT

Of course, Alfred did not know that John's act was not premeditated. He hadn't judgment enough to think things out. A scientist doesn't have to use judgment as a lawyer does. He just fools around with a lot of chemicals and things.

A man's hand slips and there you are. It is so easy to misunderstand. As John told himself afterward, Alfred was that kind of a man. He had no understanding.

At bottom that was what was the matter with him. That was why John hated him.

Alfred jumped up from the sand and struck at John. Of course John struck back. A fight started on the beach in the dark.

Both men were past the fighting age. They grunted a great deal. John got a black and blue eye. He made Alfred's nose bleed. Also he tore Alfred's clothes.

It was a good thing there was no one about. Both men belonged to athletic clubs in their respective cities. They had seen prize fights. They both tried to be scientific. Afterward each man had to laugh at the spectacle the other made of himself.

They couldn't keep it up. Pretty soon they both had to stop because they were short-winded.

They were just where they were before the

fight. Nothing had changed. The fight had settled nothing.

They went back up the stairs to John's house, neither man speaking. Then Alfred went to his room and changed his clothes. He packed his bags and went to the phone and called a cab.

He tried to appear calm. John thought he was just acting.

John was in a bathroom nursing his eye when Alfred came downstairs. He was putting cold water on his eye. When Alfred called he had to come. Both men had to smile.

However, they continued hating each other. Each man was laughing at the other.

Alfred made a suggestion. "You tell your wife," he said, "that I got a telegram and had to leave in a hurry."

The way he said "your wife" made John furious. She was just as good as any wife Alfred could get. And he had pretended to like John's wife. The skunk.

And then, almost at once, the cab came and Alfred was gone.

The house felt fine. Of course, John would have to make up a story to explain about his eye. When his wife came in he said that he and Alfred— his cousin—had been down on the beach. When they were coming up he fell and hurt his eye. "I should say you did," his wife said.

And then Alfred had got the telegram and had to leave. He had just time to catch a train.

John's wife was rather broken up. She said she had become very fond of Alfred. "I wish I had a cousin," she said.

She said that when Alfred's wife and daughter returned from Europe it would be nice to have them all for a long visit.

"Yes," John said. In spite of the inflamed eye he was so happy he would have agreed to anything. He got out of his wife's presence as soon as he could and took a walk about the house.

He thought the air of the house felt better in his lungs now that Alfred was gone.

As for the fight he was pretty sure he had got the best of it. Of course, Alfred hadn't a black eye but John had got in some good body punches.

"He'll be pretty sore in the morning," he thought, with satisfaction. As for the visit. Well, if it had to happen it wouldn't be for a long time. Alfred might have sense enough not to come.

And yet, John was a little in doubt. Alfred might bring his wife and daughter just to get even.

His wife might take a shine to John's wife.

John himself might like Alfred's daughter. He

107

was fond of young girls. That thought made him miserable again.

"That would be a pretty mess, now wouldn't it?"

It would be just like Alfred to have an attractive wife and daughter. It would be a way of showing off, making believe he was himself nice.

John thought his cousin Alfred never had been very nice. He hoped the punches he had got in on Alfred's body would make him so sore that in the morning on the train he would be unable to get out of his berth.

LIKE A QUEEN

LIKE A QUEEN

THERE is a great deal of talk made about beauty but no one defines it. It clings to some people.

Among women, now . . . the figure is something, of course, the face, the lips, the eyes.

The way the head sits on the shoulders.

The way a woman walks across the room may mean everything.

I myself have seen beauty in the most unexpected places. What has happened to me has happened also to a great many other men.

I remember a friend I had formerly in Chicago. He had something like a nervous breakdown and went down into Missouri—to the Ozark Mountains, I think.

One day he was walking on a mountain road and passed a cabin. It was a poor place with lean dogs in the yard.

There were a great many dirty children, a slovenly woman and one young girl. The young girl had gone from the cabin to a wood-pile in the yard.

She had gathered an armful of wood and was walking toward the house.

There in the road was my friend. He looked up and saw her.

There must have been something—the time, the place, the mood of the man. Ten years later he was still speaking of that woman, of her extraordinary beauty.

And there was another man. He was from Central Illinois and was raised on a farm. Later he went to Chicago and became a successful lawyer out there. He was the father of a large family.

The most beautiful woman he ever saw was with some horse traders that passed the farm where he lived as a boy. When he was in his cups one night he told me that all of his night dreams, the kind men have and that are concerned with women, were always concerned with her. He said he thought it was the way she walked. The odd part of it was she had a bruised eye. Perhaps, he said, she was the wife or the mistress of one of the horse traders.

It was a cold day and she was barefooted. The road was muddy. The horse traders, with their wagon, followed by a lot of bony horses, passed the field where the young man was at work. They did not speak to him. You know how such people stare.

And there she came along the road alone.

It may just have been another case of a rare moment for that man.

He had some sort of tool in his hand, a corn-cutting knife, he said. The woman looked at him. The horse traders looked back. They laughed. The corn-cutting knife dropped from his hand. Women must know when they register like that.

And thirty years later she was still registering.

All of which brings me to Alice.

Alice used to say the whole problem of life lay in getting past what she called the "times between."

I wonder where Alice is. She was a stout woman who had once been a singer. Then she lost her voice.

When I knew her she had blue veins spread over her red cheeks and short gray hair. She was the kind of woman who can never keep her stockings up. They were always falling down over her shoes.

She had stout legs and broad shoulders and had grown mannish as she grew older.

Such women can manage. Being a singer, of some fame once, she had made a great deal of money. She spent money freely.

For one thing, she knew a good many very rich men, bankers and others.

They took her advice about their daughters and sons. A son of such a man got into trouble. Well, he got mixed up with some woman, a waitress or a servant. The man sent for Alice. The son was resentful and determined.

The girl might be all right and then again . . .

Alice took the girl's part. "Now, you look here," she said to the banker. "You know nothing about people. Those who are interested in people do not get as rich as you have.

"And you do not undertand your son either. This affair he has got into. His finest feelings may be involved in this matter."

Alice simply swept the banker, and perhaps his wife, out of the picture. "You people." She laughed when she said that.

Of course, the son was immature. Alice did really seem to know a lot about people. She took the boy in hand—went to see the girl.

She had been through dozens of such experiences. For one thing, the boy wasn't made to feel a fool. Sons of rich men, when they have anything worth while in them, go through periods of desperation, like other young men. They go to college and read books.

Life in such men's houses is something pretty bad. Alice knew about all that. The rich man may go off and get himself a mistress—the boy's mother a lover. Such things happen.

Still the people are not so bad. There are all sorts of rich men, just as there are of poor and middle-class men.

After we became friends Alice used to explain a lot of things to me. At that time I was always worried about money. She laughed at me. "You take money too seriously," she said.

"Money is simply a way of expressing power," she said. "Men who get rich understand that. They get money, a lot of it, because they aren't afraid of it.

"The poor man or the middle-class man goes to a banker timidly. That will never do.

"If you have your own kind of power, show your hand. Make the man fear you in your own field. For example, you can write. Your rich man cannot do that. It is quite all right to exercise your own power. Have faith in yourself. If it is necessary to make him a little afraid, do so. The fact that you can do so, that you can express yourself makes you seem strange to him. Suppose you uncovered his life. The average rich man has got his rotten side and his weak side.

"And for Heaven's sake do not forget that he has his good side.

"You may go at trying to understand such a one like a fool if you want to—I mean with all sorts of preconceived notions. You could show just his rottenness, a distorted picture, ruin his vanity.

"Your poor man, or your small merchant or lawyer. Such men haven't the temptations as regards women, for example, that rich men have. There are plenty of women grafters about—some of them are physically beautiful, too.

"The poor man or the middle-class man goes about condemning the rich man for the rotten side of his life, but what rottenness is there in him?

"What secret desires has he, what greeds, buried under a placid, commonplace face?"

In the matter of the rich man's son and the woman he had got involved with, Alice in some way did manage to get at the bottom of things.

I gathered that in such affairs she took it for granted people were on the whole better than others thought them or than they thought themselves. She made the idea seem more reasonable than you would ever have thought possible.

It may be that Alice really had brains. I have met few enough people I thought had.

Most people are so one-sided, so specialized.

They can make money, or fight prize-fights or paint pictures, or they are men who are physically attractive and can get women who are physically beautiful, women who can tie men up in knots.

Or they are just plain dubs. There are plenty of dubs everywhere.

Alice swept dubs aside; she did not bother with them. She could be as cruel as a cold wind.

She got money when she wanted it. She lived around in fine houses.

Once she got a thousand dollars for me. I was in New York and broke. One day I was walking on Fifth Avenue. You know how a writer is when he cannot write. Months of that for me. My money gone. Everything I wrote was dead.

I had grown a little shabby. My hair was long and I was thin.

Lots of times I have thought of suicide when I cannot write. Every writer has such times.

Alice took me to a man in an office building. "You give this man a thousand dollars."

"What the devil, Alice? What for?"

"Because I say so. He can write, just as you can make money. He has talent. He is discouraged now, is on his uppers. He has lost his pride in life, in himself. Look at the poor fool's lips trembling."

It was quite true. I was in a bad state.

In me a great surge of love for Alice. Such a woman! She became beautiful to me.

She was talking to the man.

"The only value I can be to you is now and then when I do something like this."

"Like what?"

"When I tell you where and how you can use a thousand dollars and use it sensibly.

"To give it to a man who is as good as yourself, who is better. When he is down—when his pride is low."

Alice came from the mountains of East Tennessee. You would not believe it. When she was twenty-four, at the height of her power as a singer, she had seemed tall. The reason I speak of it was that when I knew her she appeared short—and thick.

Once I saw a photograph of her when she was young.

She was half vulgar, half lovely.

She was a mountain woman who could sing. An older man, who had been her lover, told me that at twenty-four and until she was thirty, she was like a queen.

"She walked like a queen," he said. To see her walk across a room or across the stage was something not to be forgotten.

She had lovers, a dozen of them in her time.

Then she had a bad period—for two years she drank and gambled.

Her life had apparently become useless to her and she tried to throw it away.

But people who believe in themselves make others believe. Men who had been lovers of Alice never forgot her. They never went back on her.

They said she gave them something. She was sixty when I knew her.

Once she took me up to the Adirondack Mountains. We went together in a big car with a Negro driver to a house that was half a palace. It took us two days to get there.

The whole outfit belonged to some rich man.

It was the time when Alice said she was flat. "I got you something once when you were flat, now you come with me," she had said when she saw me in New York.

She did not mean flat as regards money. She was spiritually flat.

So we went and stayed alone together in a big house. There were servants there. They had been provided for. I don't know how.

We had been there for a week and Alice had been silent. One evening we went to walk.

This was a wild country. There was a lake before the house and a mountain at the back.

It was a chilly night with a clear sky and a moon and we walked in a country road.

Then we began to climb the mountains. I can remember Alice's thick legs and her stockings coming down.

She was short-winded too. She kept stopping to puff and blow.

We plowed on silently like that. Alice, when herself, was seldom silent.

We got clear to the top of the mountain before she spoke.

She talked about what flatness is, how it hits people—floors them. Houses gone all flat, people all flat, life flat. "You think I am courageous," she said. "The hell with that. I haven't the courage of a mouse."

We sat down on a stone and she began to tell me of her life. It was an odd complex story, told in that way, in little jerks by an old woman.

There it was, the whole thing. She had come down out of the Tennessee mountains as a young girl to the city of Nashville, in Tennessee.

She got in with a singing master there who knew she could sing. "Well, I took him as a lover. He wasn't so bad."

The man spent money on her; he interested some Nashville rich man.

That man also may have been her lover. Alice did not say. There were plenty of others.

One of them—he must have amounted to less than any of the others—she had loved.

She said he was a young poet. There was something crooked in him. He did sneaking things.

That was when she was past thirty and he was twenty-five. She lost her head, she said, and of course lost him.

It was then she went to drinking, gambled, went broke. She declared she lost him because she loved him too much.

"But why wasn't he any good? Why did you have to love that sort?"

She did not know why. It had happened.

It must have been the experience that had tempered her.

But I was speaking of beauty in people, what an odd thing it is, how it appears, disappears and reappears.

I got a glimpse of it in Alice that night.

It was when we were coming back to the house, from the mountain, down the road.

We were on a hillside and stout Alice in front.

There was a muddy stretch of road and then a woods and then an open space.

The moonlight was in the open space and I was in the woods, in the darkness of the woods, but a few steps behind.

She crossed the open space ahead of me and there it was.

The thing lasted but a fleeting second. I think that all of the rich powerful men Alice had known, who had given her money, helped her when she needed help, and who have got so much from her, must have seen what I saw then. It was what the man saw in the woman by the mountain cabin and what the other man saw in the horse trader's woman in the road.

Alice when she said she was flat wasn't flat. Alice trying to shake off the memory of an unsuccessful love.

She was walking across the open moonlit stretch of road like a queen, as that man who was once her lover said she used to walk across a room or across a stage.

The mountains out of which she came as a child must have been in her at the moment, and the moon and the night.

Myself in love with her, madly, for a moment.

Is anyone in love longer than that?

Alice shaking her head slightly. There may have been a trick of the light. Her stride lengthened and she became tall, and young. I remember stopping in the woods and staring. I was like the two other men of whom I have spoken. I had a cane in my hand and it fell to the ground. I was like the man in the road and the other man in the field.

THAT SOPHISTICATION

THAT SOPHISTICATION

LONGMAN was a man I met in Paris some six or eight years ago. With his wife he had an apartment in the Boulevard Raspail. You climbed up to it with difficulty. There was no elevator.

I am not just sure where I first met him. It might have been in the studio of Madam T. Madam T. was an American woman. She came from Indianapolis. Or was it Dayton?

Anyway, she was said to have been the mistress of the Spanish poet, Sarasen. A dozen people had told me about that. It was when Sarasen was an old man.

But who was Sarasen? I had never heard of him before. I told Mabel Cathers about that. Mabel is from Chicago. She was indignant. "How should you?" she asked. "You do not know Spanish."

It was quite true. I didn't.

I suspected that Madam T. had a goiter. She wore a yellow ribbon about her neck. I was frivolous all that Summer. Being with Mabel made me so. When I was in Madam T.'s studio, I was always thinking of a song we used to sing in our Ohio town when I was a boy:

"Around her neck, she wore a yellow ribbon,
She wore it all the night and she wore it all the day.
When they asked her why in the hell she wore it,
She wore it for her lover who was far, far away."

It is all right even to have a goiter if you have as much money as Madam T. She wore exquisite gowns.

Someone said that when Sarasen was an old man she took tender and loving care of him. The old giant of literature in his dotage. I wished I could get me one like that. I told Mabel so. We were living at the same little hotel. I presume Mabel's husband was at home, in Chicago. "But you are no giant and never will be," she said smiling. She smiled so nicely I didn't mind what she said.

There was another song also in my head a lot, just at that time. It went like this:

"There's where she stays all day.
I wonder where she stays all night."

That was all I knew of the song.

No chance of keeping track of Mabel. She ran all around Paris, day and night. And she had no French. She was getting culture, sophistication. That was her purpose. She told me so herself. I liked Mabel.

But be that as it may, we will say that I did meet Harry Longman in the studio of Madam T. The house was on the Left Bank. I have forgotten the name of the street. French names never would stick in my head. There was a court, such as you see in old houses in New Orleans. In New Orleans they call them "patios." The studio occupied all the ground floor. Ralph Cook took me there the first time. But you do not know Ralph. Well, never mind.

Madam T. had bought any number of pictures by European painters, the kind that cost a lot of money. Cezannes, Von Goghs, etc. She had a lot of Monets, I remember.

Cook also had some Monets. He was the son of an American rich man.

Cook had been at Oxford, as a student, taking his degree there I think. He brought a young Englishman back with him.

The Englishman was of the healthy rosy-cheeked sort. He laughed all the time. Life was one grand show for him. He was the son of an English lord and had a title of his own but kept it out of sight. "For God's sake don't tell anybody that," he said to me, when I found it out.

He delighted in Americans. He, Cook, Mabel,

and I went to Madam T.'s together. In the large room downstairs, with the pictures on the wall, many people were gathered. They were, for the most part, mannish women and womanly men. It was to be an afternoon of poetry.

Through an open window we could see into a little court outside. In a corner there was a small structure built of stone. A stone dove perched on it. Someone told us it was a temple of love.

The Englishman liked that. The idea delighted him. He said he would like to get Cook and Mabel to go with him and worship out there. "Come on," he whispered. "Let's go and fall on our knees together. Everyone will see us. We will declare love has just come to us."

Mabel said it wasn't a subject to be dealt with lightly like that. She did not like the Englishman and told me so afterwards. "He's too frivolous about sacred things," she said. I suspected Mabel would have liked being a Madam T. herself. She hadn't the money.

"Love of what?" growled Cook. He was a big, broad-shouldered young man from somewhere in Texas. At Oxford he had made a record.

The young Englishman was a scholar, too. He seemed to me too light-minded for that, but Cook told me he was all right. "His mind sometimes lights up the whole lecture room over there at Oxford," Cook said.

On the afternoon when we went to Madam T.'s there was some sort of ceremony going on. A woman got up and read a poem. There was a great deal said about the dove and I did not exactly understand the symbolism. "What do doves do?" I asked Mabel, but she did not know. I think she was ashamed, not being better informed. There was, Cook told me afterwards, a good deal of that sort of talk going on among the English upper classes. "Well, it's sophistication, isn't it? That's what you're after, isn't it?" I asked Mabel. She treated my inquiry with scorn.

The young Englishman, Cook had got in with, had told him a good deal about it. He said that at Oxford, after he and Cook got acquainted, they used to walk about and speak of it.

The young Englishman had told Cook he thought such ideas came from living too long at one place—the English living too long in England, the French in France, the Germans in Germany. "The Russians and the Americans are still primitive peoples," he said. That made Mabel sore. It seemed, to Mabel and me, a kind of slur on our native land, the way Cook explained it.

Europeans are too tired, the Englishman had told Cook. He had a notion people are like this—

131

well, they have apparently to believe that if they move to a new place life will go better with them. A horde of people had come out of Europe to America feeling that way. Americans were still always moving about. It was certainly true of people like Mabel and myself.

The Russians too were great wanderers. They believed in the possibility of the salvation of their race through new forms of government—"all that sort of rot," the Englishman had said when he talked to Cook. You understand that Mabel and I got all this from Cook, who had certainly learned a lot since he left Texas.

The young Englishman thought the Americans an altogether primitive people. They could still believe in government. They looked toward Heaven as another and more successful America, he thought. They believed in such things as Prohibition, for example.

And it wasn't, as it sometimes seemed on the surface, merely a matter of a passion for interfering in the lives of others. There was a deep-seated and rather childish belief that all people could be saved.

But what did they mean by "being saved"?

"They meant just what they said when they used the words. They thought vaguely that a good and powerful leader would be found to lead them out of the wilderness of this life."

"Something as Moses led the Children of Israel out of Egypt, eh?"

"But he is not speaking about Jews," Mabel said. Afterwards she spoke several times about what an intellectual afternoon it was. She said she thought it was swell. Just the same there was a lot of—shall I say Krafft-Ebing—talk that got over my head and that I know Mabel didn't get. We had both missed something, not having been enough among the world-weary, I guess.

But I have got a long way from Henry Longman. Now I will come to him.

He came from Cleveland, Ohio. We saw him first, at least I did, that afternoon at Madam T.'s. He was a strange figure there. For one thing he had his wife with him. That, in that place, was strange in itself.

It seemed Cook and the young Englishman had pounced on him. I have already said that he lived in a studio apartment, on the Boulevard Raspail, on the top floor.

It was a six-storied building, six flights of stairs to climb.

Henry's wife was a big blonde and he was a big

man with a fat, red face. Cook had in some way got the low-down on him.

He came from Cleveland where he had got his wife. His father was a candy manufacturer out there.

And his wife's father was also rich.

The two fathers had been hard-working young men and had got on, in the American world. They both got rich.

Then their son and daughter had got the culture hunger. Their fathers might have been half proud of them, half ashamed. The woman, when she was in college, won a poetry prize. An American magazine, of the better class, published the poem.

Then she married the young man, the son of her father's friend. They went to live in Paris. They were conducting a salon.

They had taken that top floor, in the old building without an elevator, because it seemed to them artistic.

Their effort was to get the French to come to their place, and they did come, of course. Why not? There was food and drink, an abundance of both.

Longman and his wife spoke little French, about as much as Mabel and I. They couldn't get the hang of it.

Longman wanted us to think him an Englishman of the upper classes.

He hinted vaguely of an English family, of good blood, ruined, I gathered. "How could that be—his having all of that money?" the young Englishman asked Mabel. He, the young Englishman, had taken a fancy to Mabel. "He thinks you primitive and interesting," I kept telling her. I knew how to be nasty too. Longman's father sent him a lot of money and his wife's father sent her some money and—having all of that money—they fancied the idea of seeming poor. "We are dreadfully in debt," Longman's wife was always saying.

As she said it, we sat drinking the most expensive wines to be had in France.

They had a crowd always about—feeding people as they did, wining them.

The wine was brought in. It was opened and a glass poured for the blonde wife. She always made a wry face at the first taste. "Henry," she said sharply to her husband, "I think the wine is slightly corked." Mabel thought it was grand technique. It was a word the blonde had got hold of. When she said it her husband ran to her. We were in a large studio room, built for a painter. There was a glass roof. In the corner there was a cheap sink, such as you see in American small hotels. The husband, with a look of horror on his face, ran and poured the wine down the sink.

Expensive wine going off like that. I could see Mabel shiver. "I'll bet Mabel is a good economical housewife at home," Cook whispered to me.

Longman began to talk. He liked to give the impression that he was in Paris on some important mission, say, for the British government—for Downing Street, say. He didn't exactly say so.

And he referred to a book—one, you were to understand he was writing or had written. I couldn't get that clear. He did not say, "My Life of Napoleon" or "My Secrets of Downing Street." Just how did he get it across? There was the distinct impression left that he had written several important works. He was like an author, too modest really to refer directly to his work.

We got all that, going on day after day, month after month.

The Americans from Cleveland pretending to themselves they were important people, the guests pretending they were important.

They, the guests, pretending they had important reasons for being in Paris. A little string of lies, each telling the other a lie.

Why not? I went there on several occasions with Cook, Mabel and the young Englishman. Every evening the same thing happened.

Mabel, Cook and I got a little tired of the young

Englishman sometimes, and Mabel let him know it. It was a little hard on him and Cook. Cook had to decide whether he wanted to stick to the Englishman or to us. He stuck to us—on account of Mabel, of course.

He said it was a fair sight to see the way Mabel could cut people out of our herd. We did make up a small herd, the crowd of us at our cheap Left Bank hotel. Cook came to live there and we got three or four more—males, you may be sure.

We all used to go to Longman's a lot. There was good food and good wine and we all liked to hear Longman's wife say the wine was corked. She always said it at the first taste of the first bottle after we arrived. When someone else came in, she said it again. Mabel said she was sorry we had Prohibition in America. She would have liked, she said, to spring it on the folks at home, but it would cost too much.

She said she had come to Europe, as we all had, to get sophistication and that she thought she was getting it. Cook and I and several others tried to give her some.

She said the trouble was that the more sophistication she got the more she felt like Chicago. She said it was almost like being in Chicago, the sophistication she picked up after four or five other Americans, all of them men, began living with us at our hotel.

"I might have saved my husband all this money and got all this sophistication I'm getting, or anyway all I needed, right in Chicago," she declared several times during that Summer.

IN A STRANGE
TOWN

IN A STRANGE TOWN

A MORNING in a country town in a strange place. Everything is quiet. No, there are sounds. Sounds assert themselves. A boy whistles. I can hear the sound here, where I stand, at a railroad station. I have come away from home. I am in a strange place. There is no such thing as silence. Once I was in the country. I was at the house of a friend. "You see, there is not a sound here. It is absolutely silent." My friend said that because he was used to the little sounds of the place, the humming of insects, the sound of falling water—far-off—the faint clattering sound of a man with a machine in the distance, cutting hay. He was accustomed to the sounds and did not hear them. Here, where I am now, I hear a beating sound. Some one has hung a carpet on a clothesline and is beating it. Another boy shouts, far off— "A-ho, a-ho."

It is good to go and come. You arrive in a strange place. There is a street facing a railroad track. You get off a train with your bags. Two porters fight for possession of you and the bags as you have seen porters do with strangers in your own town.

As you stand at the station there are things to be seen. You see the open doors of the stores on the street that faces the station. People go in and out. An old man stops and looks. "Why, there is the morning train," his mind is saying to him.

The mind is always saying such things to people. "Look, be aware," it says. The fancy wants to float free of the body. We put a stop to that.

Most of us live our lives like toads, sitting perfectly still, under a plantain leaf. We are waiting for a fly to come our way. When it comes out darts the tongue. We nab it.

That is all. We eat it.

But how many questions to be asked that are never asked. Whence came the fly? Where was he going?

The fly might have been going to meet his sweetheart. He was stopped; a spider ate him.

The train on which I have been riding, a slow one, pauses for a time. All right, I'll go to the Empire House. As though I cared.

It is a small town—this one—to which I have come. In any event I'll be uncomfortable here. There will be the same kind of cheap brass beds as at the last place to which I went unexpectedly like this—

with bugs in the bed perhaps. A traveling salesman will talk in a loud voice in the next room. He will be talking to a friend, another traveling salesman. "Trade is bad," one of them will say. "Yes, it's rotten."

There will be confidences about women picked up—some words heard, others missed. That is always annoying.

But why did I get off the train here at this particular town? I remember that I had been told there was a lake here—that there was fishing. I thought I would go fishing.

Perhaps I expected to swim. I remember now.

"Porter, where is the Empire House? Oh, the brick one. All right, go ahead. I'll be along pretty soon. You tell the clerk to save me a room, with a bath, if they have one."

I remember what I was thinking about. All my life, since that happened, I have gone off on adventures like this. A man likes to be alone sometimes.

Being alone doesn't mean being where there are no people. It means being where people are all strangers to you.

There is a woman crying there. She is getting old, that woman. Well, I am myself no longer young.

See how tired her eyes are. There is a younger woman with her. In time that younger woman will look exactly like her mother.

She will have the same patient, resigned look. The skin will sag on her cheeks that are plump now. The mother has a large nose and so has the daughter.

There is a man with them. He is fat and has red veins in his face. For some reason I think he must be a butcher.

He has that kind of hands, that kind of eyes.

I am pretty sure he is the woman's brother. Her husband is dead. They are putting a coffin on the train.

They are people of no importance. People pass them casually. No one has come to the station to be with them in their hour of trouble. I wonder if they live here. Yes, of course they do. They live somewhere, in a rather mean little house, at the edge of town, or perhaps outside the town. You see the brother is not going away with the mother and daughter. He has just come down to see them off.

They are going, with the body, to another town where the husband, who is dead, formerly lived.

The butcher-like man has taken his sister's arm. That is a gesture of tenderness. Such people make such gestures only when someone in the family is dead.

The sun shines. The conductor of the train is walking along the station platform and talking to the station-master. They have been laughing loudly, having their little joke.

That conductor is one of the jolly sort. His eyes twinkle, as the saying is. He has his little joke with every station-master, every telegraph operator, baggage man, express man, along the way. There are all kinds of conductors of passenger trains.

There, you see, they are passing the woman whose husband has died and is being taken away somewhere to be buried. They drop their jokes, their laughter. They become silent.

A little path of silence made by that woman in black and her daughter and the fat brother. The little path of silence has started with them at their house, has gone with them along streets to the railroad station, will be with them on the train and in the town to which they are going. They are people of no importance, but they have suddenly become important.

They are symbols of Death. Death is an important, a majestic thing, eh?

How easily you can comprehend a whole life, when you are in a place like this, in a strange place, among strange people. Everything is so much like other towns you have been in. Lives are made up of little series of circumstances. They repeat themselves, over and over, in towns everywhere, in cities, in all countries.

They are of infinite variety. In Paris, when I was there last year, I went into the Louvre. There were men and women there, making copies of the works of the old masters that were hung on the walls. They were professional copyists.

They worked painstakingly, were trained to do just that kind of work, very exactly.

And yet no one of them could make a copy. There were no copies made.

The little circumstances of no two lives anywhere in the world are just alike.

You see I have come over into a hotel room now, in this strange town. It is a country-town hotel. There are flies in here. A fly has just alighted on this paper on which I have been writing these impressions. I stopped writing and looked at the fly. There must be billions of flies in the world and yet, I dare say, no two of them are alike.

The circumstances of their lives are not just alike.

I think I must come away from my own place on trips, such as I am on now, for a specific reason.

At home I live in a certain house. There is my own household, the servants, the people of my household. I am a professor of philosophy in a college in my town, hold a certain definite position there, in the town life and in the college life.

Conversations in the evening, music, people coming into our house.

Myself going to a certain office, then to a class room where I lecture, seeing people there.

I know some things about these people. That is the trouble with me perhaps. I know something but not enough.

My mind, my fancy, becomes dulled looking at them.

I know too much and not enough.

It is like a house in the street in which I live. There is a particular house in that street—in my home town—I was formerly very curious about. For some reason the people who lived in it were recluses. They seldom came out of their house and hardly ever out of the yard, into the street.

Well, what of all that?

My curiosity was aroused. That is all.

I used to walk past the house with something strangely alive in me. I had figured out this much. An old man with a beard and a white-faced woman

147

lived there. There was a tall hedge and once I looked through. I saw the man walking nervously up and down, on a bit of lawn, under a tree. He was clasping and unclasping his hands and muttering words. The doors and shutters of the mysterious house were all closed. As I looked, the old woman with the white face opened the door a little and looked out at the man. Then the door closed again. She said nothing to him. Did she look at him with love or with fear in her eyes? How do I know? I could not see.

Another time I heard a young woman's voice, although I never saw a young woman about the place. It was evening and the woman was singing— a rather sweet young woman's voice it was.

There you are. That is all. Life is more like that than people suppose. Little odd fragmentary ends of things. That is about all we get. I used to walk past that place all alive, curious. I enjoyed it. My heart thumped a little.

I heard sounds more distinctly, felt more.

I was curious enough to ask my friends along the street about the people.

"They're queer," people said.

Well, who is not queer?

The point is that my curiosity gradually died.

I accepted the queerness of the life of that house. It became a part of the life of my street. I became dulled to it.

I have become dulled to the life of my own house, or my street, to the lives of my pupils.

"Where am I? Who am I? Whence came I?" Who asks himself these questions any more?

There is that woman I saw taking her dead husband away on the train. I saw her only for a moment before I walked over to this hotel and came up to this room (an entirely commonplace hotel room it is) but here I sit, thinking of her. I reconstruct her life, go on living the rest of her life with her.

Often I do things like this, come off alone to a strange place like this. "Where are you going?" my wife says to me. "I am going to take a bath," I say.

My wife thinks I am a bit queer too, but she has grown used to me. Thank God, she is a patient and a good-natured woman.

"I am going to bathe myself in the lives of people about whom I know nothing."

I will sit in this hotel until I am tired of it and then I will walk in strange streets, see strange houses, strange faces. People will see me.

Who is he?

He is a stranger.

That is nice. I like that. To be a stranger sometimes, going about in a strange place, having no business there, just walking, thinking, bathing myself.

To give others, the people here in this strange place, a little jump at the heart too—because I am something strange.

Once, when I was a young man I would have tried to pick up a girl. Being in a strange place, I would have tried to get my jump at the heart out of trying to be with her.

Now I do not do that. It is not because I am especially faithful—as the saying goes—to my wife, or that I am not interested in strange and attractive women.

It is because of something else. It may be that I am a bit dirty with life and have come here, to this strange place, to bathe myself in strange life and get clean and fresh again.

And so I walk in such a strange place. I dream. I let myself have fancies. Already I have been out into the street, into several streets of this town and have walked about. I have aroused in myself a little stream of fresh fancies, clustered about strange lives, and as I walked, being a stranger, going along slowly, carrying a cane, stopping to look into stores, stopping to look into the windows of houses and into gardens, I have, you see, aroused in others something of the same feeling that has been in me.

I have liked that. Tonight, in the houses of this town, there will be something to speak of.

"There was a strange man about. He acted queerly. I wonder who he was."

"What did he look like?"

An attempt to delve into me too, to describe me. Pictures being made in other minds. A little current of thoughts, fancies, started in others, in me too.

I sit here in this room in this strange town, in this hotel, feeling oddly refreshed. Already I have slept here. My sleep was sweet. Now it is morning and everything is still. I dare say that, some time today, I shall get on another train and go home.

But now I am remembering things.

Yesterday, in this town, I was in a barber shop. I got my hair cut. I hate getting my hair cut.

"I am in a strange town, with nothing to do, so I'll get my hair cut," I said to myself as I went in.

A man cut my hair. "It rained a week ago," he

said. "Yes," I said. That is all the conversation there was between us.

However, there was other talk in that barber shop, plenty of it.

A man had been here in this town and had passed some bad checks. One of them was for ten dollars and was made out in the name of one of the barbers in the shop.

The man who passed the checks was a stranger, like myself. There was talk of that.

A man came in who looked like President Coolidge and had his hair cut.

Then there was another man who came for a shave. He was an old man with sunken cheeks and for some reason looked like a sailor. I dare say he was just a farmer. This town is not by the sea.

There was talk enough in there, a whirl of talk.

I came out thinking.

Well, with me it is like this. A while ago I was speaking of a habit I have formed of going suddenly off like this to some strange place. "I have been doing it ever since it happened," I said. I used the expression "it happened."

Well, what happened?

Not so very much.

A girl got killed. She was struck by an automobile. She was a girl in one of my classes.

She was nothing special to me. She was just a girl—a woman, really—in one of my classes. When she was killed I was already married.

She used to come into my room, into my office. We used to sit in there and talk.

We used to sit and talk about something I had said in my lecture.

"Did you mean this?"

"No, that is not exactly it. It is rather like this."

I suppose you know how we philosophers talk. We have almost a language of our own. Sometimes I think it is largely nonsense.

I would begin talking to that girl—that woman —and on and on I would go. She had gray eyes. There was a sweet serious look on her face.

Do you know, sometimes, when I talked to her like that (it is, I am pretty sure, all nonsense), well, I thought . . .

Her eyes seemed to me sometimes to grow a little larger as I talked to her. I had a notion she did not hear what I said.

I did not care much.

I talked so that I would have something to say.

Sometimes, when we were together that way, in my office in the college building, there would come odd times of silence.

No, it was not silence. There were sounds.

There was a man walking in a hallway, in the college building outside my door. Once when this happened I counted the man's footsteps. Twenty-six, twenty-seven, twenty-eight.

I was looking at the girl—the woman—and she was looking at me.

You see I was an older man. I was married.

I am not such an attractive man. I did, however, think she was very beautiful. There were plenty of young fellows about.

I remember now that when she had been with me like that—after she had left—I used to sit sometimes for hours alone in my office, as I have been sitting here, in this hotel room, in a strange town.

I sat thinking of nothing. Sounds came in to me. I remembered things of my boyhood.

I remembered things about my courtship and my marriage. I sat like that dumbly, a long time.

I was dumb, but I was at the same time more aware than I had ever been in my life.

It was at that time I got the reputation with my wife of being a little queer. I used to go home, after sitting dumbly like that, with that girl, that woman, and I was even more dumb and silent when I got home.

"Why don't you talk?" my wife said.

"I'm thinking," I said.

I wanted her to believe that I was thinking of my work, my studies. Perhaps I was.

Well, the girl, the woman, was killed. An automobile struck her when she was crossing a street. They said she was absent-minded—that she walked right in front of a car. I was in my office, sitting there, when a man, another professor, came in and told me. "She is quite dead, was quite dead when they picked her up," he said.

"Yes." I dare say he thought I was pretty cold and unsympathetic—a scholar, eh, having no heart.

"It was not the driver's fault. He was quite blameless."

"She walked right out in front of the car?"

"Yes."

I remember that at the moment I was fingering a pencil. I did not move. I must have been sitting like that for two or three hours.

I got out and walked. I was walking when I saw a train. So I got on.

Afterward I telephoned to my wife. I don't remember what I told her at that time.

It was all right with her. I made some excuse. She is a patient and a good-natured woman. We have four children. I dare say she is absorbed in the children.

I came to a strange town and I walked about there. I forced myself to observe the little details of life. That time I stayed three or four days and then I went home.

At intervals I have been doing the same thing ever since. It is because at home I grow dull to little things. Being in a strange place like this makes me more aware. I like it. It makes me more alive.

So you see, it is morning and I have been in a strange town, where I know no one and where no one knows me.

As it was yesterday morning, when I came here, to this hotel room, there are sounds. A boy whistles in the street. Another boy, far off, shouts "A-ho."

There are voices in the street, below my window, strange voices. Some one, somewhere in this town, is beating a carpet. I hear the sound of the arrival of a train. The sun is shining.

IN A STRANGE TOWN

I may stay here in this town another day or I may go on to another town. No one knows where I am. I am taking this bath in life, as you see, and when I have had enough of it I shall go home feeling refreshed.

THESE MOUNTAINEERS

THESE MOUNTAINEERS

W H E N I had lived in the Southwest Virginia mountains for some time, people of the North, when I went up there, used to ask me many questions about the mountain people. They did it whenever I went to the city. You know how people are. They like to have everything ticketed.

The rich are so and so, the poor are so and so, the politicians, the people of the Western Coast. As though you could draw one figure and say—"there it is. That's it."

The men and women of the mountains were what they were. They were people. They were poor whites. That certainly meant that they were white and poor. Also they were mountaineers.

After the factories began to come down into this country, into Virginia, Tennessee and North Carolina, a lot of them went, with their families, to work in the factories and to live in mill towns. For a time all was peace and quiet, and then strikes broke out. Every one who reads newspapers knows about that.

There was a lot of writing in newspapers about these mountain people. Some of it was pretty keen.

But there had been a lot of romancing about them before that. That sort of thing never did any one much good.

So I was walking alone in the mountains and had got down into what in the mountain country is called "a hollow." I was lost. I had been fishing for trout in mountain streams and was tired and hungry. There was a road of a sort I had got into. It would have been difficult to get a car over that road. "This ought to be a good whisky-making country," I thought.

In the hollow along which the road went I came to a little town. Well, now, you would hardly call it a town. There were six or eight little unpainted frame houses and, at a cross roads, a general store.

The mountains stretched away, above the poor little houses. On both sides of the road were the magnificent hills. You understand, when you have been down there, why they are called the "Blue Ridge." They are always blue, a glorious blue. What a country it must have been before the lumber men came! Over near my place in the mountains men were always talking of the spruce forests of former days. Many of them worked in the lumber camps. They speak of soft moss into which a man sank almost to the knees, the silence of the forest, the great trees.

The great forest is gone now, but the young trees are growing. Much of the country will grow nothing but timber.

The store before which I stood that day was closed, but an old man sat on a little porch in front. He said that the storekeeper also carried the mail and was out on his route but that he would be back and open his store in an hour or two.

I had thought I might at least get some cheese and crackers or a can of sardines.

The man on the porch was old. He was an evil-looking old man. He had gray hair and a gray beard and might have been seventy, but I could see that he was a tough-bodied old fellow.

I asked my way back over the mountain to the main road and had started to move off up the hollow when he called to me. "Are you the man who has moved in here from the North and has built a house in here?"

There is no use my trying to reproduce the mountain speech. I am not skilled at it.

The old man invited me to his house to eat. "You don't mind eating beans, do you?" he asked.

I was hungry and would be glad to have beans. I would have eaten anything at the moment. He

163

said he hadn't any woman, that his old woman was dead. "Come on," he said, "I think I can fix you up."

We went up a path, over a half mountain and into another hollow, perhaps a mile away. It was amazing. The man was old. The skin on his face and neck was wrinkled like an old man's skin and his legs and body were thin, but he walked at such a pace that to follow him kept me panting.

It was a hot, still day in the hills. Not a breath of air stirred. That old man was the only being I saw that day in that town. If any one else lived there he had kept out of sight.

The old man's house was on the bank of another mountain stream. That afternoon, after eating with him, I got some fine trout out of the stream.

But this isn't a fishing story. We went to his house.

It was dirty and small and seemed about to fall down. The old man was dirty. There were layers of dirt on his old hands and on his wrinkled neck. When we were in the house, which had but one room on the ground floor, he went to a small stove. "The fire is out," he said. "Do you care if the beans are cold?"

"No," I said. By this time I did not want any beans and wished I had not come. There was something evil about this old mountain man. Surely the romancers could not have made much out of him.

Unless they played on the Southern hospitality chord. He had invited me there. I had been hungry. The beans were all he had.

He put some of them on a plate and put them on a table before me. The table was a home-made one covered with a red oil cloth, now quite worn. There were large holes in it. Dirt and grease clung about the edges of the holes. He had wiped the plate, on which he had put the beans, on the sleeve of his coat.

But perhaps you have not eaten beans prepared in the mountains, in the mountain way. They are the staff of life down there. Without beans there would be no life in some of the hills. The beans are, when prepared by a mountain woman and served hot, often delicious. I do not know what they put in them or how they cook them, but they are unlike any beans you will find anywhere else in the world.

As Smithfield ham, when it is real Smithfield ham, is unlike any other ham.

But beans cold, beans dirty, beans served on a plate wiped on the sleeve of that coat . . .

I sat looking about. There was a dirty bed in the room in which we sat and an open stairway, leading up to the room above.

Some one moved up there. Some one walked barefooted across the floor. There was silence for a time and then it happened again.

You must get the picture of a very hot still place between hills. It was June. The old man had become silent. He was watching me. Perhaps he wanted to see whether or not I was going to scorn his hospitality. I began eating the beans with a dirty spoon. I was many miles away from any place I had ever been before.

And then there was that sound again. I had got the impression that the old man had told me his wife was dead, that he lived alone.

How did I know it was a woman upstairs? I did know.

"Have you got a woman up there?" I asked. He grinned, a toothless malicious grin, as though to say, "Oh, you're curious, eh?"

And then he laughed, a queer cackle.

"She ain't mine," he said.

We sat in silence after that and then there was the sound again. I heard bare feet walking across a plank floor.

Now the feet were descending the crude open stairs. Two legs appeared, two thin, young girl's legs.

She didn't look to be over twelve or thirteen.

166

She came down, almost to the foot of the stairs, and then stopped and sat down.

How dirty she was, how thin, what a wild look she had! I have never seen a wilder-looking creature. Her eyes were bright. They were like the eyes of a wild animal.

And, at that, there was something about her face. In many of these young mountain faces there is a look it is difficult to explain—it is a look of breeding, of aristocracy. I know no other word for the look.

And she had it.

And now the two were sitting there, and I was trying to eat. Suppose I rose and threw the dirty beans out at the open door. I might have said, "Thank you, I have enough." I didn't dare.

But perhaps they weren't thinking of the beans. The old man began to speak of the girl, sitting ten feet from him, as though she were not there.

"She ain't mine," he said. "She came here. Her pop died. She ain't got any one."

I am making a bad job of trying to reproduce his speech.

He was giggling now, a toothless old man's giggle. "Ha, she won't eat.

"She's a hell cat," he said.

He reached over and touched **me on the** arm.

167

"You know what. She's a hell cat. You couldn't satisfy her. She had to have her a man.

"And she got one too."

"Is she married?" I asked, half whispering the words, not wanting her to hear.

He laughed at the idea. "Ha. Married, eh?"

He said it was a young man from farther down the hollow. "He lives here with us," the old man said laughing, and as he said it the girl rose and started back up the stairs. She had said nothing, but her young eyes had looked at us, filled with hatred. As she went up the stairs the old man kept laughing at her, his queer, high-pitched, old man's laugh. It was really a giggle. "Ha, she can't eat. When she tries to eat she can't keep it down. She thinks I don't know why. She's a hell cat. She would have a man and now she's got one.

"Now she can't eat."

I fished in the creek in the hollow during the afternoon and toward evening began to get trout. They were fine ones. I got fourteen of them and got back over a mountain and into the main road before dark.

What took me back into the hollow I don't know. The face of the girl possessed me.

And then there was good trout fishing there. That stream at least had not been fished out.

168

When I went back I put a twenty-dollar bill in my pocket. "Well," I thought—I hardly know what I did think. There were notions in my head, of course.

The girl was very, very young.

"She might have been kept there by that old man," I thought, "and by some young mountain rough. There might be a chance for her."

I thought I would give her the twenty dollars. "If she wants to get out perhaps she can," I thought. Twenty dollars is a lot of money in the hills.

It was just another hot day when I got in there again and the old man was not at home. At first I thought there was no one there. The house stood alone by a hardly discernible road and near the creek. The creek was clear and had a swift current. It made a chattering sound.

I stood on the bank of the creek before the house and tried to think.

"If I interfere . . ."

Well, let's admit it. I was a bit afraid. I thought I had been a fool to come back.

And then the girl suddenly came out of the house and came toward me. There was no doubt about it. She was that way. And unmarried, of course.

At least my money, if I could give it to her,

would serve to buy her some clothes. The ones she had on were very ragged and dirty. Her feet and legs were bare. It would be winter by the time the child was born.

A man came out of the house. He was a tall young mountain man. He looked rough. "That's him," I thought. He said nothing.

He was dirty and unkempt as the old man had been and as the child was.

At any rate she was not afraid of me. "Hello, you are back here," she said. Her voice was clear.

Just the same I saw the hatred in her eyes. I asked about the fishing. "Are the trout biting?" I asked. She had come nearer me now, and the young man had slouched back into the house.

Again I am at a loss about how to reproduce her mountain speech. It is peculiar. So much is in the voice.

Hers was cold and clear and filled with hatred.

"How should I know? He" (indicating with a gesture of her hand the tall slouching figure who had gone into the house) "is too damn' lazy to fish.

"He's too damn' lazy for anything on earth."

She was glaring at me.

"Well," I thought, "I will at least try to give her the money." I took the bill in my hand and held it toward her. "You will need some clothes," I said. "Take it and buy yourself some clothes."

It may have been that I had touched her mountain pride. How am I to know? The look of hatred in her eyes seemed to grow more intense.

"You go to hell," she said. "You get out of here. And don't you come back in here again."

She was looking hard at me when she said this. If you have never known such people, who live like that, "on the outer fringe of life," as we writers say (you may see them sometimes in the tenement districts of cities as well as in the lonely and lovely hills) —such a queer look of maturity in the eyes of a child. . . .

It sends a shiver through you. Such a child knows too much and not enough. Before she went back into the house she turned and spoke to me again. It was about my money.

She told me to put it somewhere, I won't say where. The most modern of modern writers has to use some discretion.

Then she went into the house. That was all. I left. What was I to do? After all, a man looks after his hide. In spite of the trout I did not go fishing in that hollow again.

A SENTIMENTAL
JOURNEY

A SENTIMENTAL JOURNEY

M Y friend David, with his wife, Mildred, came to live in the hills. She was a delicate little woman. I used to go often to the cabin they had rented. Although David is a scholar, he and a mountain man, named Joe, a man much older than David, became friends. I sat in their cabin one evening, after I had first met David, while he told me the story. Joe was not there and Mildred was in the kitchen at work.

Joe is a thin mountain man of forty with the straight wiry figure of a young boy. David spoke of the first time he ever saw the man. He said: "I remember that he frightened me. It was a day last Fall, when we had first come in here, and I was on the gray horse riding the hills.

"I was a little nervous. You know how it is. Romantic tales of mountain men shooting strangers from behind trees or from wooded mountain-sides floated through my mind. Suddenly, out of an old timber road, barely discernible, leading off up into the hills, he emerged.

"He was mounted on a beautifully gaited but

bony bay horse, and while I admired the horse's gait I feared the rider.

"What a fierce-looking man! Stories of men taken for Federal agents and killed by such fellows on lonely roads became suddenly real. His face was long and lean and he had a huge nose. His thin cheeks had not been shaved for weeks. He had on, I remember, an old wide-brimmed black hat, pulled well down over his eyes, and the eyes were cold and gray. The eyes stared at me. They were as cold as the gray sky overhead.

"Out of the thick golden-brown trees, well up the side of the mountain down which Joe had just come, I saw a thin column of smoke floating up into the sky. 'He has a still up there,' I thought. I felt myself in a dangerous position.

"Joe rode past me without speaking. My horse stood motionless in the road. I did not dare take my eyes off the man. 'He will shoot me in the back,' I thought. What a silly notion! My hands were trembling. 'Well,' I thought. 'Howdy,' said Joe.

"Stopping the bay horse he waited for me and we rode together down the mountain-side. He was curious about me. As to whether he had a still concealed in the woods I do not now know and I haven't asked. No doubt he had.

"And so Joe the mountain-man rode with me

to my house here. (It was a log cabin built on the bank of a creek.) Mildred was inside cooking dinner. When we got to the little bridge that crosses the creek I looked at the man who had ridden beside me for half an hour without speaking and he looked at me. ''Light,' I said, 'and come in and eat.' We walked across the bridge toward the house. The night was turning cold. Before we entered the house he touched my arm gently with his long bony hand. He made a motion for me to stop and took a bottle from his coat pocket. I took a sip, but it was raw new stuff and burned my throat. It seemed to me that Joe took a half pint in one great gulp. 'It's new, he'll get drunk,' I thought, 'he'll raise hell in the house.' I was afraid for Mildred. She had been ill. That was the reason we had come up here, into this country.

"We were sitting here in the house by the fireplace here and could look through that open door. While we ate Mildred was nervous and kept looking at Joe with frightened eyes. There was the open door there, and Joe looked through it and into his hills. Darkness was coming on fast and in the hills a strong wind blew, but it did not come down into this valley. The air above was filled with floating yellow and red leaves. The room here was heavy with late Fall smells and the smell of moon whisky. That was Joe's breath.

"He was curious about my typewriter and the row of books on the shelves up there along the wall, but the fact that we were living in this old log house put him at his ease. We were not too grand. Mountain men are, as a rule, as you know, uncommunicative, but it turned out that Joe is a talker. He wanted to talk. He said that he had been wanting to come and see us for a long time. Someone had told him we were from distant parts, that we had seen the ocean and foreign lands. He had himself always wanted to go wandering in the big world but had been afraid. The idea of his being frightened of anything seemed absurd. I glanced at Mildred and we both smiled. We were feeling easier.

"And now Joe began to talk to us of his one attempt to go out of these mountains and into the outside world. It hadn't been successful. He was a hill man and could not escape the hills, had been raised in the hills and had never learned to read or write. He got up and fingered one of my books cautiously and then sat down again. 'Oh, Lord,' I thought, 'the man is lucky.' I had just read the book he had touched and after the glowing blurb on the jacket it had been a bitter disappointment.

"He told us that he had got married when he was sixteen and suggested vaguely that there was a reason. There often is, I guess, among these mountain people. Although he is yet a young man he is the father of fourteen children. Back in the hills somewhere he owned a little strip of land, some twenty acres, on which he raised corn. Most of the corn, I fancy, goes into whisky. A man who has fourteen children and but twenty acres of land has to scratch hard to live. I imagined that the coming of Prohibition and the rise in the price of moon has been a big help to him.

"That first evening his being with us started his mind reaching out into the world. He began talking of the journey he had once taken—that time he tried to escape from the hills.

"It was when he had been married but a short time and had but six children. Suddenly he decided to go out of the hills and into the broad world. Leaving his wife and five of the children at home in his mountain cabin, he set out—taking with him the oldest, a boy of seven.

"He said he did it because his corn crop had failed and his two hogs had died. It was an excuse. He really wanted to travel. He had a bony horse, and taking the boy on behind him he set out over the hills. I gathered that he had taken the boy because he was afraid he would be too lonely in the big world without some of his family. It was late Fall and the boy had no shoes.

"They went through the hills and down into a plain and then on into other hills and came at last to a coal-mining town where there were also factories. It was a large town. Joe got a job in the mines at once and he got good wages. It must have been a good year. He had never made so much money before. He told us, as though it were a breath-taking statement, that he made four dollars a day.

"It did not cost him much to live. He and the boy slept on the floor in a miner's cabin. The house in which they slept must have belonged to an Italian. Joe spoke of the people with whom he lived as 'Tallies.'

"And there was Joe, the mountain man, in the big world and he was afraid. There were the noises in the house at night. Joe and the boy were accustomed to the silence of the hills. In another room, during the evenings, men gathered and sat talking. They drank and began to sing. Sometimes they fought. They seemed as strange and terrible to Joe and his son as these mountain people had seemed at first to Mildred and myself. At night he came home from the mine, having bought some food at a store, and then he and the boy sat on a bench and ate. There were tears of loneliness in the boy's eyes. Joe hadn't put him in school. None of his children ever went to school. He was ashamed. He was only staying in the mining country to make money. His curiosity about the outside world was quite gone. How sweet these distant hills now seemed to him!

"On the streets of the mining town crowds of men were going along. There was a huge factory with grim-looking walls. What a noise it made! It kept going night and day. The air was filled with black smoke. Freight trains were always switching up and down a siding near the house where Joe and the boy lay on the floor, under the patched quilts they had brought with them from the hills.

"And then winter came. It snowed and froze and then snowed again. In the hills now the snow would be ten feet deep in places. Joe was hungry for its whiteness. He was working in the mines but he said he did not know how to get his money at the week's end. He was shy about asking. You had to go to a certain office where they had your name on a book. Joe said he did not know where it was.

"At last he found out. What a lot of money he had! Clutching it in his hand he went to the miner's house and got the boy. They had left the horse with a small farmer across the plain at the place where the hills began.

"They went there that evening, wading through the deep snow. It was bitter cold. I asked Joe if he had got shoes for the boy and he said 'no.' He said that by the time he got ready to start back into the hills it was night and the stores were closed. He figured he had enough money to buy a hog and some corn. He could go back to making whisky, back to these hills. Both he and the boy were half insane with desire.

"He cut up one of the quilts and made a covering for the boy's feet. Sitting in our house here, as the darkness came, he described the journey.

"It was an oddly dramatic recital. Joe had the gift. There was really no necessity for his starting off in such a rush. He might have waited until the roads were broken after the great snow.

"The only explanation he could give us was that he could not wait and the boy was sick with loneliness.

"And so, since he had been a boy, Joe had wanted to see the outside world, and now, having seen it, he wanted back his hills. He spoke of the happiness of himself and the boy trudging in the darkness in the deep snow.

"There was his woman in his cabin some eighty miles away in the hills. What of her? No one in the family could read or write. She might be getting out of wood. It was absurd. Such mountain women can fell trees as well as a man.

"It was all sentimentality on Joe's part. He

knew that. At midnight he and the boy reached the cabin where they had left the horse and getting on the horse rode all of that night. When they were afraid they would freeze they got off the horse and struggled forward afoot. Joe said it warmed them up.

"They kept it up like that all the way home. Occasionally they came to a mountain cabin where there was a fire.

"Joe said the trip took three days and three nights and that he lost his way but he had no desire to sleep. The boy and the horse had, however, to have rest. At one place, while the boy slept on the floor of a mountain house before a fire and the horse ate and rested in a stable, Joe sat up with another mountain man and played cards from after midnight until four in the morning. He said he won two dollars.

"All the people in the mountain cabins on the way welcomed him and there was but one house where he had trouble. Looking at Mildred and myself, Joe smiled when he spoke of that night. It was when he had lost his way and had got down out of the hills and into a valley. The people of that house were outsiders. They were not hill people. I fancy they were afraid of Joe, as Mildred and I had been afraid, and that being afraid they had wanted to close the door on him and the boy.

"When he stopped at the house and called from the road a man put his head out at a window and told him to go away. The boy was almost frozen. Joe laughed. It was two in the morning.

"What he did was to take the boy in his arms and walk to the front door. Then he put his shoulder to the door and pushed. He got in. There was a little fireplace in a large front room and he went through the house to the back door and got wood.

"The man and his wife, dressed, Joe said, like city folks—that is to say, evidently in night clothes, pajamas perhaps—came to the door of a bedroom and looked at him. What he looked like, standing there in the firelight with the old hat pulled down over his face—the long lean face and the cold eyes— you may imagine.

"He stayed in the house three hours, warming himself and the boy. He went into a stable and fed the horse. The people in the house never showed themselves again. They had taken the one look at Joe and then going quickly back into the bedroom had closed and locked the door.

"Joe was curious. He said it was a grand house. I gathered it was much grander than my place. The whole inside of the house, he said, was like one big grand piece of furniture. Joe went into the kitchen but would not touch the food he found. He said he reckoned the people of the house were higher toned than we were. They were, he said, so high and mighty that he would not touch their food. What they were doing with such a house in that country he did not know. In some places, in the valleys among the hills, he said high-toned people like us were now coming in. He looked at Mildred and smiled when he said that.

"And, anyway, as Joe said, the people of the grand house evidently did not have any better food than he sometimes had at home. He had been curious and had gone into the kitchen and the pantry to look. I looked at Mildred. I was glad he had seemed to like our food.

"And so Joe and the boy were warmed and the horse was fed and they left the house as they had found it, the two strange people, who might also have heard or read tales of the dangerous character of mountain people, trembling in the room in which they had locked themselves.

"They got, Joe said, to their own house late on the next evening and they were almost starved. The snow had grown deeper. After the first heavy snow there had been a rain followed by sleet and then came more snow. In some of the mountain passes he and the boy had to go ahead of the horse, breaking the way.

"They got home at last and Joe did nothing but sleep for two days. He said the boy was all right. He also slept. Joe tried to explain to us that he had taken the desperate trip out of the mining country back into his own hills in such a hurry because he was afraid his wife, back in her cabin in the hills, would be out of firewood, but when he said it he had to smile.

" 'Pshaw,' he said, grinning sheepishly, 'there was plenty of wood in the house.' "

A JURY CASE

A JURY CASE

T H E Y had a still up in the mountains. There were
three of them. They were all tough.

What I mean is they were not men to fool with
—at least two of them weren't.

First of all, there was Harvey Groves. Old man
Groves had come into the mountain country thirty
years before, and had bought a lot of mountain land.

He hadn't a cent and had only made a small pay-
ment on the land.

Right away he began to make moon whisky. He
was one of the kind that can make pretty fair whisky
out of anything. They make whisky out of potatoes,
buckwheat, rye, corn or whatever they can get—
the ones who really know how. One of that kind
from here was sent to prison. He make whisky out
of the prunes they served the prisoners for breakfast—anyway, he called it whisky. Old man Groves
used to sell his whisky down at the lumber mills.
There was a big cutting going on over on Briar Top
Mountain.

They brought the lumber down the mountain to a town called Lumberville.

Old Groves sold his whisky to the lumberjacks and the manager of the mill got sore. He had old Groves into his office and tried to tell him what was what.

Instead, old Groves told him something. The manager said he would turn old Groves up. What he meant was that he would send the Federal men up the mountains after him, and old Groves told the manager that if a Federal man showed up in his hills he would burn the lumber stacked high about the mills at Lumberville.

He said it and he meant it and the mill manager knew he meant it.

The old man got away with that. He stayed up in his hills and raised a large family. Those at home were all boys. Every one about here speaks of the Groves girls, but what became of them I've never heard. They are not here now.

Harvey Groves was a tall, raw-boned young man with one eye. He lost the other one in a fight. He began drinking and raising the devil all over the hills when he was little more than a boy and after the old man died of a cancer, and the old woman died and the land was divided among the sons and sold, and he got his share, he blew it in gambling and drinking.

He went moonshining when he was twenty-five. Cal Long and George Small went in with him. They all chipped in to buy the still.

Nowadays you can make moon whisky in a small still—it's called "over-night stuff"—about fourteen gallons to the run, and you make a run in one night.

You can sell it fast. There are plenty of men to buy and run it into the coal mining country over east of here. It's pretty raw stuff.

Cal Long, who went in with Harvey, is a big man with a beard. He is as strong as an ox. They don't make them any meaner. He seems a peaceful enough man, when he isn't drinking, but when he starts to drink, look out. He usually carries a long knife and he has cut several men pretty badly. He has been in jail three times.

The third man in the party was George Small. He used to come by our house—lived out our way for a time. He is a small nervous-looking young man who worked, until last Summer, on the farm of old man Barclay. One day last Fall, when I was over on the Barclay road and was sitting under a bridge, fishing, George came along the road.

What was the matter with him that time I've never found out.

I was sitting in silence under the bridge and he came along the road making queer movements with his hands. He was giving them a dry wash. His lips were moving. The road makes a turn right beyond the bridge and I could see him coming for almost a half mile before he got to the bridge. I was under the bridge and could see him without his seeing me. When he got close I heard his words. "Oh, my God, don't let me do it," he said. He kept saying it over and over. He had got married the Spring before. He might have had some trouble with his wife. I remember her as a small, red-haired woman. I saw the pair together once. George was carrying their baby in his arms and we stopped to talk. The woman moved a little away. She was shy as most mountain women are. George showed me the baby—not more than two weeks old—and it had a wrinkled little old face. It looked ages older than the father and mother but George was fairly bursting with pride while I stood looking at it.

How he happened to go in with men like Harvey Groves and Cal Long is a wonder to me, and why they wanted him is another wonder.

I had always thought of George as a country neurotic—the kind you so often see in cities. He always seemed to me out of place among the men of these hills.

He might have fallen under the influence of Cal Long. A man like Cal likes to bully people physically. Cal liked to bully them spiritually too.

Luther Ford told me a tale about Cal and George. He said that one night in the Winter Cal went to George Small's house—it is a tumble-down little shack up in the hills—and called George out. The two men went off together to town and got drunk. They came back about two o'clock in the morning and stood in the road before George's house. I have already told you something about the wife. Luther said that at that time she was sick. She was going to have another baby. A neighbor had told Luther Ford. It was a queer performance, one of the kind of things that happen in the country and that give you the creeps.

He said the two men stood in the road before the house cursing the sick woman inside.

Little nervous George Small walking up and down the road in the snow, cursing his wife—Cal Long egging him on. George strutting like a little rooster. It must have been a sight to see and to make you a little sick seeing. Luther Ford said just hearing about it gave him a queer feeling in the pit of his stomach.

This Spring early these three men went in together, making whisky.

Between Cal and Harvey Groves it was a case of dog eat dog. They had bought the still together, each putting in a third of its cost, and then, one night after they had made and sold two runs, Harvey stole the still from the other two.

Of course Cal set out to get him for that.

There wasn't any law he and George Small could evoke—or whatever it is you do with a law when you use it to get some man.

It took Cal a week to find out where Harvey had hidden, and was operating, the still, and then he went to find George.

He wanted to get Harvey, but he wanted to get the still too.

He went to George Small's house and tramped in. George was sitting there and when he saw Cal was frightened stiff. His wife, thinner than ever since her second child was born and half sick, was lying on a bed. In these little mountain cabins there is often but one room and they cook, eat and sleep in it—often a big family.

When she saw Cal, George's wife began to cry and, very likely, George wanted to cry too.

Cal sat down in a chair and took a bottle out of his pocket. George's wife says he had been drinking. He gave George a drink, staring at him hard when he offered it, and George had to take it.

George took four or five stiff drinks, not looking again at Cal or at his wife, who lay on the bed moaning and crying, and Cal never said a word.

Then suddenly George jumped up—his hands not doing the dry wash now—and began swearing at his wife.

"You keep quiet, God damn you!" he yelled.

Then he did an odd thing. There were only two chairs in the cabin and Cal Long had been sitting on one and George on the other. When Cal got up George took the chairs, one at a time, and going outside smashed them to splinters against a corner of the cabin.

Cal Long laughed at that. Then he told George to get his shotgun.

George did get it. It was hanging on a hook in the house and was loaded, I presume, and the two went away together into the woods.

Harvey Groves had got bold. He must have thought he had Cal Long bluffed. That's the weakness of these tough men. They never think any one else is as tough as they are.

Harvey had set the still up in a tiny, half-broken-down old house, on what had once been his father's land, and was making a daylight run.

He had two guns up there but never got a chance to use either of them.

Cal and George must have just crept up pretty close to the house in the long grass and weeds.

They got up close, George with the gun in his hands, and then Harvey came to the door of the house. He may have heard them. Some of these mountain men, who have been law-breakers since they were small boys, have sharp ears and eyes.

There must have been a terrific moment. I've talked with Luther Ford and several others about it. We are all, of course, sorry for George.

Luther, who is something of a dramatist, likes to describe the scene. His version is, to be sure, all a matter of fancy. When he tells the story he kneels in the grass with a stick in his hand. He begins to tremble and the end of the stick wobbles about. He has taken a distant tree for the figure of Harvey Groves, now dead. When he tells of the scene in that way, all of us standing about and, in spite of the ridiculous figure Luther cuts, a little breathless, he goes on for perhaps five seconds, wobbling the stick about, apparently utterly helpless and frightened and then his figure suddenly seems to stiffen and harden.

Luther could do it better if he wasn't built as he is—long and loose-jointed, whereas George Small, whose part in the tragedy he is playing, is small, and, as I have said, nervous and rather jerky.

But Luther does what he can, saying in a low voice to us others standing and looking, "Now, Cal Long has touched me on the shoulder."

The idea, you understand, is that the two men have crept up to the lonely little mountain house in the late afternoon, George Small creeping ahead with the heavily loaded shotgun in his hands, really being driven forward by Cal Long, creeping at his heels, a man, Luther explains, simply too strong for him, and that, at the fatal moment, when they faced Harvey Groves, and I presume had to shoot or be shot, and George weakened, Cal Long just touched George on the shoulder.

The touch, you see, according to Luther's notion, was a command.

It said, "Shoot!" and George's body stiffened, and he shot.

He shot straight, too.

There was a piece of sheet-iron lying by the door of the house. What it was doing there I don't know. It may have been some part of the stolen still. In the fraction of a second that Harvey Groves had to live he snatched it up and tried to hold it up before his body.

The shot tore right through the metal and

through Harvey Groves' head and through a board back of his head. The gun may not have been loaded when George Small brought it from his house. Cal Long may have loaded it.

Anyway Harvey Groves is dead. He died, Luther says, like a rat, in a hole—just pitched forward and flopped around a little and died. How a rat in a hole, when he dies, can do much flopping around I don't know.

After the killing, of course, Cal and George ran, but before they did any running Cal took the gun out of George Small's hands and threw it in the grass.

That, Luther says, was to show just whose gun did the killing.

They ran and, of course, they hid themselves.

There wasn't any special hurry. They had shot Harvey Groves in that lonely place and he might not have been found for days but that George Small's wife, being sick and nervous, just as he is, ran down into town, after Cal and George had left their place, and went around to the stores crying and wringing her hands like a little fool, telling every one that her husband and Cal Long were going to kill some one.

Of course, that stirred every one up.

There must have been people in town who

knew that Cal and George and Harvey had been in together and what they had been up to.

They found the body the next morning—the shooting had happened about four in the afternoon —and they got George Small that next afternoon.

Cal Long had stayed with him until he got tired of it and then had left him to shift for himself. They haven't got Cal yet. A lot of people think they never will get him. "He's too smart," Luther Ford says.

They got George sitting beside a road over on the other side of the mountains. He says Cal Long stopped an automobile driving past, a Ford, stopped the driver with a revolver he had in his pocket all the time.

They haven't even found the man who drove the Ford. It may be he was some one who knows Cal and is afraid.

Anyway, they have got George Small in jail over at the county seat and he tells every one he did the killing and sits and moans and rubs his funny little hands together and keeps saying over and over, "God, don't let me do it," just as he did that day when he crossed the bridge, long before he got into this trouble, and I was under the bridge fishing and saw and heard him. I presume they'll hang him, or electrocute him—whichever it is they do in this State —when the time for his trial comes.

And his wife is down with a high fever, and, Luther says, has gone clear off her nut.

But Luther, who acts the whole thing out so dramatically whenever he can get an audience, and who is something of a prophet, says that if they have to get a jury from this county to try George Small, even though the evidence is all against him, he thinks the jury will just go it blind and bring in a verdict of not guilty.

He says, anyway, that is what he would do, and others, who see him acting the thing out and who know Cal Long and Harvey Groves and George Small better than I do, having lived longer in this county and having known them all since they were boys, say the same thing.

It may be true. As for myself—being what I am, hearing and seeing all this . . .

How do I know what I think?

It's a matter, of course, the jury will have to decide.

ANOTHER WIFE

ANOTHER WIFE

H E thought himself compelled to say something special to her—knowing her—loving her—wanting her. What he thought was that perhaps she wanted him too, or she wouldn't have spent so much time with him. He wasn't exactly modest.

After all, he was modest enough. He was quite sure several men must have loved her and thought it not unlikely she had experimented with at least a few of them. It was all imagined. Seeing her about had started his mind—his thoughts—racing. "Modern women, of her class, used to luxuries, sensitive, are not going to miss anything, even though they don't take the final plunge into matrimony as I did when I was younger," he thought. The notion of sin had, for him, more or less been taken out of that sort of thing. "What you try to do, if you are a modern woman with any class to you, is to try to use your head," he thought.

He was forty-seven and she ten years younger. His wife had been dead two years.

For the last month she had been in the habit

of coming down from her mother's country house to his cabin two or three evenings a week. She might have invited him up the hill to the house—would have invited him oftener—but that she preferred having him, his society, in his own cabin. The family, her family, had simply left the whole matter to her, let her manage it. She lived in her mother's country house, with the mother and two younger sisters— both unmarried. They were delightful people to be with. It was the first summer he had been up in that country and he had met them after he took the cabin. He ate at a hotel nearly a half mile away. Dinner was served early. By getting right back he could be sure of being at home if she decided to stroll down his way.

Being with her, at her mother's house with the others, was fun, of course, but some one was always dropping in. He thought the sisters liked to tease her and him by arranging things that would tie them down.

It was all pure fancy, just a notion. Why should they be concerned about him?

What a whirlpool of notions were stirred up in him that Summer by the woman! He thought about her all the time, having really nothing else to do. Well, he had come to the country to rest. His one son was at a Summer school.

"It's like this—here I am, practically alone. What am I letting myself in for? If she, if any of the women of that family, were of the marrying sort, she would have made a marriage with a much more likely man long ago." Her younger sisters were so considerate in their attitude toward her. There was something tender, respectful, teasing, too, about the way they acted when he and she were together.

Little thoughts kept running through his head. He had come to the country because something inside him had let down. It might have been his forty-seven years. A man like himself, who had begun life as a poor boy, worked himself up in his profession, who had become a physician of some note—well, a man dreams his dreams, he wants a lot.

At forty-seven he is likely, at any moment, to run into a slump.

You won't get half, a third of what you wanted, in your work, in life. What's the use going on? These older men who keep on striving like young men, what about them? They are a little childlike, immature, really.

A great man might go on like that, to the bitter end, to the brink of the grave, but who, having any sense, any head, wants to be a great man? What is called a great man may be just an illusion in people's minds. Who wants to be an illusion?

Thoughts like that, driving him out of the city —to rest. God knows it would have been a mistake if she hadn't been there. Before he met her and before she got into the unwomanly habit of coming to see him in his own cabin during the long Summer evenings, the country, the quiet of the country, was dreadful.

"It may be she only comes down here to me because she is bored. A woman like that, who has known many men, brilliant men, who has been loved by men of note. Still, why does she come? I'm not so gay. It's sure she doesn't think me witty or brilliant."

She was thirty-seven, a bit inclined to extremes in dress, plump, to say the least. Life didn't seem to have quieted her much.

When she came down to his cabin, at the edge of the stream facing the country road, she dropped onto a couch by the door and lit a cigarette. She had lovely ankles. Really, they were beautiful ankles.

The door was open and he sat by a chair near a table. He burned an oil-lamp. The cabin door was left open. Country people went past.

"The trouble with all this silly business about resting is that a man thinks too much. A physician in practice—people coming in, other people's troubles—hasn't time."

Women had come to him a good deal—married and unmarried women. One woman—she was married—wrote him a long letter after he had been treating her for three years. She had gone with her husband to California. "Now that I am away from you, will not see you again, I tell you frankly I love you."

What an idea!

"You have been patient with me for these three years, have let me talk to you. I have told you all the intimate things of my life. You have been always a little aloof and wise."

What nonsense! How could he have stopped the woman's talking intimately? There was more of that sort of thing in the letter. The doctor did not feel he had been specially wise with the woman patient. He had really been afraid of her. What she had thought was aloofness was really fright.

Still, he had kept the letter—for a time. He destroyed it finally because he did not want it to fall accidentally into his wife's hands.

A man likes to feel he has been of some account to some one.

The doctor, say, in the cabin, the new woman near him. She was smoking a cigarette. It was Saturday evening. People—men, women and children—were going along the country road toward a mountain town. Presently the country women and children would be coming back without the men. On Saturday evenings nearly all the mountain-men got drunk.

You come from the city and, because the hills are green, the water in mountain streams clear, you think the people of the hills must be at the bottom clear and sweet.

Now the country people in the road were turning to stare into the cabin at the woman and the doctor. On a previous Saturday evening, after midnight, the doctor had been awakened by a noisy drunken conversation carried on in the road. It had made him tremble with wrath. He had wanted to rush out into the road and fight the drunken country men, but a man of forty-seven . . . The men in the road were sturdy young fellows.

One of the men was telling the others in a loud voice that the woman now on the couch near the doctor—that she was really a loose city woman. He had used a very distasteful word and had sworn to the others that, before the Summer was over, he intended having her himself.

It was just crude drunken talk. The fellow had

laughed when he said it, and the others had laughed. It was a drunken man trying to be funny.

If the woman with the doctor had known—if he told her? She would only have smiled.

How many thoughts about her in the doctor's head! He felt sure she had never cared much what others thought. They had been sitting like that, she smoking her after-dinner cigarette, he thinking, but a few minutes. In her presence, thoughts came quickly, dancing through his head. He wasn't used to such a multitude of thoughts. When he was in town—in practice—there were plenty of things to think of other than women, being in love with some woman.

With his wife it had never been like that. She had never excited him, except at first physically. After that he had just accepted her. "There are many women. She is my woman. She is rather nice, does her share of the job"—that sort of an attitude.

When she had died it had left a gaping hole in his life.

"That may be what is the matter with me."

"This other woman is a different sort surely. The way she dresses; her ease with people. Such people, having money always, from the first, a secure position in life—they just go along, quite sure of themselves, never afraid."

His early poverty had, the doctor thought, taught him a good many things he was glad to know. It had taught him other things not so good to know. Both he and his wife had always been a little afraid of people—of what people might think—of his standing in his profession. He had married a woman who also came from a poor family. She was a nurse before she married him. The woman now in the room with him got up from the couch and threw the end of her cigarette into the fireplace. "Let's walk," she said.

When they got out into the road and had turned away from the town and her mother's house, standing on a hill between his cabin and town, another person on the road behind might have thought him the distinguished one. She was a bit too plump— not tall enough—while he had a tall, rather slender figure and walked with a free, easy carriage. He carried his hat in his hand. His thick graying hairs added to his air of distinction.

The road grew more uneven and they walked close to each other. She was trying to tell him something. There had been something he had determined to tell her—on this very evening. What was it?

Something of what the woman in California had tried to tell him in that foolish letter—not doing very well at it—something to the effect that she—this new woman—met while he was off guard, resting—was aloof from himself—unattainable—but that he found himself in love with her.

If she found, by any odd chance, that she wanted him, then he would try to tell her.

After all, it was foolish. More thoughts in the doctor's head. "I can't be very ardent. This being in the country—resting—away from my practice—is all foolishness. My practice is in the hands of another man. There are cases a new man can't understand.

"My wife who died—she didn't expect much. She had been a nurse, was brought up in a poor family, had always had to work, while this new woman . . ."

There had been some kind of nonsense the doctor had thought he might try to put into words. Then he would get back to town, back to his work. "I'd much better light out now, saying nothing."

She was telling him something about herself. It was about a man she had known and loved, perhaps.

Where had he got the notion she had had several lovers? He had merely thought—well, that sort of woman—always plenty of money—being always with clever people.

When she was younger she had thought for a time she would be a painter, had studied in New York and Paris.

She was telling him about an Englishman—a novelist.

The devil—how had she known his thoughts?

She was scolding him. What had he said?

She was talking about such people as himself, simple, straight, good people, she called them, people who go ahead in life, doing their work, not asking much.

She, then, had illusions as he had.

"Such people as you get such ideas in your heads —silly notions."

Now she was talking about herself again.

"I tried to be a painter. I had such ideas about the so-called big men in the arts. You, being a doctor, without a great reputation—I have no doubt you have all sorts of ideas about so-called great doctors, great surgeons."

Now she was telling what happened to her. There had been an English novelist she had met in Paris. He had an established reputation. When he seemed attracted to her she had been much excited.

The novelist had written a love story and she had read it. It had just a certain tone. She had always thought that above everything in life she wanted a love affair in just that tone. She had tried it with the writer of the story and it had turned out nothing of the sort.

It was growing dark in the road. Laurels and elders grew on a hillside. In the half-darkness he could see faintly the little hurt shrug of her shoulders.

Had all the lovers he had imagined for her, the brilliant, witty men of the great world, been like that? He felt suddenly as he had felt when the drunken country men talked in the road. He wanted to hit someone with his fist, in particular he wanted to hit a novelist—preferably an English novelist—or a painter or musician.

He had never known any such people. There weren't any about. He smiled at himself, thinking: "When that country man talked I sat still and let him." His practice had been with well-to-do merchants, lawyers, manufacturers, their wives and families.

Now his body was trembling. They had come to a small bridge over a stream, and suddenly, without premeditation, he put his arm about her.

There had been something he had planned to tell her. What was it? It was something about himself. "I am no longer young. What I could have to offer you would not be much. I cannot offer it to such a one as yourself, to one who has known great people, been loved by witty, brilliant men."

There had no doubt been something of the sort he had foolishly thought of saying. Now she was in his arms in the darkness on the bridge. The air was heavy with Summer perfumes. She was a little heavy—a real armful. Evidently she liked having him hold her thus. He had thought, really, she might like him but have at the same time a kind of contempt for him.

Now he had kissed her. She liked that too. She moved closer and returned the kiss. He leaned over the bridge. It was a good thing there was a support of some sort. She was sturdily built. His first wife, after thirty, had been fairly plump, but this new woman weighed more.

And now they were again walking in the road. It was the most amazing thing. There was something quite taken for granted. It was that he wanted her to marry him.

Did he? They walked along the road toward his cabin and there was in him the half-foolish, half-joyful mood a boy feels walking in the darkness the first time, alone with a girl.

A quick rush of memories, evenings as a boy and as a young man remembered.

Does a man ever get too old for that? A man like himself, a physician, should know more about things. He was smiling at himself in the darkness—feeling foolish, feeling frightened, glad. Nothing definite had been said.

It was better at the cabin. How nice it had been of her to have no foolish, conventional fears about coming to see him! She was a nice person. Sitting alone with her in the darkness of the cabin he realized that they were at any rate both mature—grown up enough to know what they were doing.

Did they?

When they had returned to the cabin it was quite dark and he lighted an oil-lamp. It all got very definite very rapidly. She had another cigarette and sat as before, looking at him. Her eyes were gray. They were gray, wise eyes.

She was realizing perfectly his discomfiture. The eyes were smiling—being old eyes. The eyes were saying: "A man is a man and a woman is a woman. You can never tell how or when it will happen. You are a man and, although you think yourself a practical, unimaginative man, you are a good deal of a boy. There is a way in which any woman is older than any man and that is the reason I know."

Never mind what her eyes were saying. The

doctor was plainly fussed. There had been a kind of speech he had intended making. It may have been he had known, from the first, that he was caught.

"O Lord, I won't get it in now."

He tried, haltingly, to say something about the life of a physician's wife. That he had assumed she might marry him, without asking her directly, seemed a bit rash. He was assuming it without intending anything of the sort. Everything was muddled.

The life of a physician's wife—a man like himself—in general practice—wasn't such a pleasant one. When he had started out as a physician he had really thought, some time, he might get into a great position, be some kind of a specialist.

But now—

Her eyes kept on smiling. If he was muddled she evidently wasn't. "There is something definite and solid about some women. They seem to know just what they want," he thought.

She wanted him.

What she said wasn't much. "Don't be so foolish. I've waited a long time for just you."

That was all. It was final, absolute—terribly disconcerting too. He went and kissed her, awkwardly. Now she had the air that had from the first disconcerted him, the air of worldliness. It might not be anything but her way of smoking a cigarette—an undoubtedly good, although rather bold, taste in clothes.

His other wife never seemed to think about clothes. She hadn't the knack.

Well, he had managed again to get her out of his cabin. It might be she had managed. His first wife had been a nurse before he married her. It might be that women who have been nurses should not marry physicians. They have too much respect for physicians, are taught to have too much respect. This one, he was quite sure, would never have too much respect.

It was all, when the doctor let it sink in, rather nice. He had taken the great leap and seemed suddenly to feel solid ground under his feet. How easy it had been!

They were walking along the road toward her mother's house. It was dark and he could not see her eyes.

He was thinking—

"Four women in her family. A new woman to be the mother of my son." Her mother was old and quiet and had sharp gray eyes. One of the younger

DEATH IN THE WOODS

sisters was a bit boyish. The other one—she was the handsome one of the family—sang Negro songs.

They had plenty of money. When it came to that his own income was quite adequate.

It would be nice, being a kind of older brother to the sisters, a son to her mother. O Lord!

They got to the gate before her mother's house and she let him kiss her again. Her lips were warm, her breath fragrant. He stood, still embarrassed, while she went up a path to the door. There was a light on the porch.

There was no doubt she was plump, solidly built. What absurd notions he had had!

Well, it was time to go on back to his cabin. He felt foolishly young, silly, afraid, glad.

"O Lord—I've got me a wife, another wife, a new one," he said to himself as he went along the road in the darkness. How glad and foolish and frightened he still felt! Would he get over it after a time?

A MEETING SOUTH

A MEETING SOUTH

H E told me the story of his ill fortune—a crack-up in an airplane—with a very gentlemanly little smile on his very sensitive, rather thin, lips. Such things happened. He might well have been speaking of another. I liked his tone and I liked him.

This happened in New Orleans, where I had gone to live. When he came, my friend, Fred, for whom he was looking, had gone away, but immediately I felt a strong desire to know him better and so suggested we spend the evening together. When we went down the stairs from my apartment I noticed that he was a cripple. The slight limp, the look of pain that occasionally drifted across his face, the little laugh that was intended to be jolly, but did not quite achieve its purpose, all these things began at once to tell me the story I have now set myself to write.

"I shall take him to see Aunt Sally," I thought. One does not take every caller to Aunt Sally. However, when she is in fine feather, when she has taken a fancy to her visitor, there is no one like her.

Although she has lived in New Orleans for thirty years, Aunt Sally is Middle Western, born and bred.

However I am plunging a bit too abruptly into my story.

First of all I must speak more of my guest, and for convenience's sake I shall call him David. I felt at once that he would be wanting a drink and, in New Orleans—dear city of Latins and hot nights— even in Prohibition times such things can be managed. We achieved several and my own head became somewhat shaky but I could see that what we had taken had not affected him. Evening was coming, the abrupt waning of the day and the quick smoky soft-footed coming of night, characteristic of the semi-tropic city, when he produced a bottle from his hip pocket. It was so large that I was amazed. How had it happened that the carrying of so large a bottle had not made him look deformed? His body was very small and delicately built. "Perhaps, like the kangaroo, his body has developed some kind of a natural pouch for taking care of supplies," I thought. Really he walked as one might fancy a kangaroo would walk when out for a quiet evening stroll. I went along thinking of Darwin and the marvels of Prohibition. "We are a wonderful people, we Americans," I thought. We were both in fine humor and had begun to like each other immensely.

He explained the bottle. The stuff, he said, was made by a Negro man on his father's plantation somewhere over in Alabama. We sat on the steps of a vacant house deep down in the old French Quarter of New Orleans—the Vieux Carré—while he explained that his father had no intention of breaking the law—that is to say, in so far as the law remained reasonable. "Our nigger just makes whisky for us," he said. "We keep him for that purpose. He doesn't have anything else to do, just makes the family whisky, that's all. If he went selling any, we'd raise hell with him. I dare say Dad would shoot him if he caught him up to any such unlawful trick, and you bet, Jim, our nigger, I'm telling you of, knows it too.

"He's a good whisky-maker, though, don't you think?" David added. He talked of Jim in a warm friendly way. "Lord, he's been with us always, was born with us. His wife cooks for us and Jim makes our whisky. It's a race to see which is best at his job, but I think Jim will win. He's getting a little better all the time and all of our family—well, I reckon we just like and need our whisky more than we do our food."

Do you know New Orleans? Have you lived there in the Summer when it is hot, in the Winter

223

when it rains, and through the glorious late Fall days? Some of its own, more progressive, people scorn it now. In New Orleans there is a sense of shame because the city is not more like Chicago or Pittsburgh.

It, however, suited David and me. We walked slowly, on account of his bad leg, through many streets of the Old Town, Negro women laughing all around us in the dusk, shadows playing over old buildings, children with their shrill cries dodging in and out of old hallways. The old city was once almost altogether French, but now it is becoming more and more Italian. It however remains Latin. People live out of doors. Families were sitting down to dinner within full sight of the street—all doors and windows open. A man and his wife quarreled in Italian. In a patio back of an old building a Negress sang a French song.

We came out of the narrow little streets and had a drink in front of the dark cathedral and another in a little square in front. There is a statue of General Jackson, always taking off his hat to Northern tourists who in Winter come down to see the city. At his horse's feet an inscription—"The Union must and will be preserved." We drank solemnly to that declaration and the general seemed to bow a bit lower. "He was sure a proud man,"

David said, as we went over toward the docks to sit in the darkness and look at the Mississippi. All good New Orleanians go to look at the Mississippi at least once a day. At night it is like creeping into a dark bedroom to look at a sleeping child—something of that sort—gives you the same warm nice feeling, I mean. David is a poet and so in the darkness by the river we spoke of Keats and Shelley, the two English poets all good Southern men love.

All of this, you are to understand, was before I took him to see Aunt Sally.

Both Aunt Sally and myself are Middle Western- ers. We are but guests down here, but perhaps we both in some queer way belong to this city. Some- thing of the sort is in the wind. I don't quite know how it has happened.

A great many Northern men and women come down our way and, when they go back North, write things about the South. The trick is to write nigger stories. The North likes them. They are so amusing. One of the best-known writers of nigger stories was down here recently and a man I know, a Southern man, went to call on him. The writer seemed a bit nervous. "I don't know much about the South or Southerners," he said. "But you have your reputa- tion," my friend said. "You are so widely known as a writer about the South and about Negro life."

The writer had a notion he was being made sport of. "Now look here," he said, "I don't claim to be a highbrow. I'm a business man myself. At home, up North, I associate mostly with business men and when I am not at work I go out to the country club. I want you to understand I am not setting myself up as a highbrow.

"I give them what they want," he said. My friend said he appeared angry. "About what now, do you fancy?" he asked innocently.

However, I am not thinking of the Northern writer of Negro stories. I am thinking of the Southern poet, with the bottle clasped firmly in his hands, sitting in the darkness beside me on the docks facing the Mississippi.

He spoke at some length of his gift for drinking. "I didn't always have it. It is a thing built up," he said. The story of how he chanced to be a cripple came out slowly. You are to remember that my own head was a bit unsteady. In the darkness the river, very deep and very powerful off New Orleans, was creeping away to the gulf. The whole river seemed to move away from us and then to slip noiselessly into the darkness like a vast moving sidewalk.

When he had first come to me, in the late afternoon, and when we had started for our walk together I had noticed that one of his legs dragged as we went along and that he kept putting a thin hand to an equally thin cheek.

Sitting over by the river he explained, as a boy would explain when he has stubbed his toe running down a hill.

When the World War broke out he went over to England and managed to get himself enrolled as an aviator, very much, I gathered, in the spirit in which a countryman, in a city for a night, might take in a show.

The English had been glad enough to take him on. He was one more man. They were glad enough to take any one on just then. He was small and delicately built but after he got in he turned out to be a first-rate flyer, serving all through the War with a British flying squadron, but at the last got into a crash and fell.

Both legs were broken, one of them in three places, the scalp was badly torn and some of the bones of the face had been splintered.

They had put him into a field hospital and had patched him up. "It was my fault if the job was rather bungled," he said. "You see it was a field hospital, a hell of a place. Men were torn all to pieces, groaning and dying. Then they moved me back to a base hospital and it wasn't much better. The fellow who had the bed next to mine had shot

himself in the foot to avoid going into a battle. A
lot of them did that, but why they picked on their
own feet that way is beyond me. It's a nasty place,
full of small bones. If you're ever going to shoot
yourself don't pick on a spot like that. Don't pick on
your feet. I tell you it's a bad idea.

"Anyway, the man in the hospital was always
making a fuss and I got sick of him and the place
too. When I got better I faked, said the nerves of my
leg didn't hurt. It was a lie, of course. The nerves
of my leg and of my face have never quit hurting.
I reckon maybe, if I had told the truth, they might
have fixed me up all right."

I got it. No wonder he carried his drinks so well.
When I understood, I wanted to keep on drinking
with him, wanted to stay with him until he got tired
of me as he had of the man who lay beside him in
the base hospital over there somewhere in France.

The point was that he never slept, could not
sleep, except when he was a little drunk. "I'm a
nut," he said smiling.

It was after we got over to Aunt Sally's that he
talked most. Aunt Sally had gone to bed when we
got there, but she got up when we rang the bell
and we all went to sit together in the little patio back
of her house. She is a large woman with great arms
and rather a paunch, and she had put on nothing

but a light flowered dressing-gown over a thin, ridiculously girlish, nightgown. By this time the moon had come up and, outside, in the narrow street of the Vieux Carré, three drunken sailors from a ship in the river were sitting on a curb and singing a song,

> *"I've got to get it,*
> *You've got to get it,*
> *We've all got to get it*
> *In our own good time."*

They had rather nice boyish voices and every time they sang a verse and had done the chorus they all laughed together heartily.

In Aunt Sally's patio there are many broad-leafed banana plants and a Chinaberry tree throwing its soft purple shadows on a brick floor.

As for Aunt Sally, she is as strange to me as he was. When we came and when we were all seated at a little table in the patio, she ran into her house and presently came back with a bottle of whisky. She, it seemed, had understood him at once, had understood without unnecessary words that the little Southern man lived always in the black house of pain, that whisky was good to him, that it quieted his throbbing nerves, temporarily at least. "Everything is temporary, when you come to that," I can fancy Aunt Sally saying.

We sat for a time in silence, David having shifted his allegiance and taken two drinks out of Aunt Sally's bottle. Presently he rose and walked up and down the patio floor, crossing and re-crossing the network of delicately outlined shadows on the bricks. "It's really all right, the leg," he said, "something just presses on the nerves, that's all." In me there was a self-satisfied feeling. I had done the right thing. I had brought him to Aunt Sally. "I have brought him to a mother." She has always made me feel that way since I have known her.

And now I shall have to explain her a little. It will not be so easy. That whole neighborhood in New Orleans is alive with tales concerning her.

Aunt Sally came to New Orleans in the old days, when the town was wild, in the wide-open days. What she had been before she came no one knew, but anyway she opened a place. That was very, very long ago when I was myself but a lad, up in Ohio. As I have already said Aunt Sally came from somewhere up in the Middle-Western country. In some obscure subtle way it would flatter me to think she came from my State.

The house she had opened was one of the older

places in the French Quarter down here, and when she had got her hands on it, Aunt Sally had a hunch. Instead of making the place modern, cutting it up into small rooms, all that sort of thing, she left it just as it was and spent her money rebuilding falling old walls, mending winding broad old stairways, repairing dim high-ceilinged old rooms, soft-colored old marble mantels. After all, we do seem attached to sin and there are so many people busy making sin unattractive. It is good to find someone who takes the other road. It would have been so very much to Aunt Sally's advantage to have made the place modern, that is to say, in the business she was in at that time. If a few old rooms, wide old stairways, old cooking ovens built into the walls, if all these things did not facilitate the stealing in of couples on dark nights, they at least did something else. She had opened a gambling and drinking house, but one can have no doubt about the ladies stealing in. "I was on the make all right," Aunt Sally told me once.

She ran the place and took in money, and the money she spent on the place itself. A falling wall was made to stand up straight and fine again, the banana plants were made to grow in the patio, the Chinaberry tree got started and was helped through the years of adolescence. On the wall the lovely Rose of Montana bloomed madly. The fragrant Lantana grew in a dense mass at a corner of the wall.

When the Chinaberry tree, planted at the very center of the patio, began to get up into the light it filled the whole neighborhood with fragrance in the Spring.

Fifteen, twenty years of that, with Mississippi River gamblers and race-horse men sitting at tables by windows in the huge rooms upstairs in the house that had once, no doubt, been the town house of some rich planter's family—in the boom days of the Forties. Women stealing in, too, in the dusk of evenings. Drinks being sold. Aunt Sally raking down the kitty from the game, raking in her share, quite ruthlessly.

At night, getting a good price too from the lovers. No questions asked, a good price for drinks. Moll Flanders might have lived with Aunt Sally. What a pair they would have made! The Chinaberry tree beginning to be lusty. The Lantana blossoming —in the Fall the Rose of Montana.

Aunt Sally getting hers. Using the money to keep the old house in fine shape. Salting some away all the time.

A motherly soul, good, sensible Middle-Western woman, eh? Once a race-horse man left twenty-four thousand dollars with her and disappeared. No one

232

knew she had it. There was a report the man was dead. He had killed a gambler in a place down by the French Market and while they were looking for him he managed to slip in to Aunt Sally's and leave his swag. Some time later a body was found floating in the river and it was identified as the horseman but in reality he had been picked up in a wire-tapping haul in New York City and did not get out of his Northern prison for six years.

When he did get out, naturally, he skipped for New Orleans. No doubt he was somewhat shaky. She had him. If he squealed there was a murder charge to be brought up and held over his head. It was night when he arrived and Aunt Sally went at once to an old brick oven built into the wall of the kitchen and took out a bag. "There it is," she said. The whole affair was part of the day's work for her in those days.

Gamblers at the tables in some of the rooms upstairs, lurking couples, from the old patio below the fragrance of growing things.

When she was fifty, Aunt Sally had got enough and had put them all out. She did not stay in the way of sin too long and she never went in too deep, like that Moll Flanders, and so she was all right and sitting pretty. "They wanted to gamble and drink and play with the ladies. The ladies liked it all right.

I never saw none of them come in protesting too much. The worst was in the morning when they went away. They looked so sheepish and guilty. If they felt that way, what made them come? If I took a man, you bet I'd want him and no monkey-business or nothing doing.

"I got a little tired of all of them, that's the truth." Aunt Sally laughed. "But that wasn't until I had got what I went after. Oh, pshaw, they took up too much of my time, after I got enough to be safe."

Aunt Sally is now sixty-five. If you like her and she likes you she will let you sit with her in her patio gossiping of the old times, of the old river days. Perhaps—well, you see there is still something of the French influence at work in New Orleans, a sort of matter-of-factness about life—what I started to say is that if you know Aunt Sally and she likes you, and if, by chance, your lady likes the smell of flowers growing in a patio at night—really, I am going a bit too far. I only meant to suggest that Aunt Sally at sixty-five is not harsh. She is a motherly soul.

We sat in the garden talking, the little Southern poet, Aunt Sally and myself—or rather they talked and I listened. The Southerner's great-grandfather was English, a younger son, and he came over here to make his fortune as a planter, and did it. Once he and his sons owned several great plantations with slaves, but now his father had but a few hundred acres left, about one of the old houses—somewhere over in Alabama. The land is heavily mortgaged and most of it has not been under cultivation for years. Negro labor is growing more and more expensive and unsatisfactory since so many Negroes have run off to Chicago, and the poet's father and the one brother at home are not much good at working the land. "We aren't strong enough and we don't know how," the poet said.

The Southerner had come to New Orleans to see Fred, to talk with Fred about poetry, but Fred was out of town. I could only walk about with him, help him drink his home-made whisky. Already I had taken nearly a dozen drinks. In the morning I would have a headache.

I drew within myself, listening while David and Aunt Sally talked. The Chinaberry tree had been so and so many years growing—she spoke of it as she might have spoken of a daughter. "It had a lot of different sicknesses when it was young, but it pulled through." Some one had built a high wall on one side of her patio so that the climbing plants did not get as much sunlight as they needed. The banana plants, however, did very well and now the Chinaberry tree was big and strong enough to take care of itself. She kept giving David drinks of whisky and he talked.

He told her of the place in his leg where something, a bone perhaps, pressed on the nerve, and of the place on his left cheek. A silver plate had been set under the skin. She touched the spot with her fat old fingers. The moonlight fell softly down on the patio floor. "I can't sleep except somewhere out of doors," David said.

He explained how that, at home on his father's plantation, he had to be thinking all day whether or not he would be able to sleep at night.

"I go to bed and then I get up. There is always a bottle of whisky on the table downstairs and I take three or four drinks. Then I go out doors." Often very nice things happened.

"In the Fall it's best," he said. "You see the niggers are making molasses." Every Negro cabin on the place had a little clump of ground back of it where cane grew and in the Fall the Negroes were making their 'lasses. "I take the bottle in my hand and go into the fields, unseen by the niggers. Having the bottle with me, that way, I drink a good deal and then lie down on the ground. The mosquitoes bite me some, but I don't mind much. I reckon I get drunk enough not to mind. The little pain makes a kind of rhythm for the great pain—like poetry.

236

"In a kind of shed the niggers are making the 'lasses, that is to say, pressing the juice out of the cane and boiling it down. They keep singing as they work. In a few years now I reckon our family won't have any land. The banks could take it now if they wanted it. They don't want it. It would be too much trouble for them to manage, I reckon.

"In the Fall, at night, the niggers are pressing the cane. Our niggers live pretty much on 'lasses and grits.

"They like working at night and I'm glad they do. There is an old mule going round and round in a circle and beside the press a pile of the dry cane. Niggers come, men and women, old and young. They build a fire outside the shed. The old mule goes round and round.

"The niggers sing. They laugh and shout. Sometimes the young niggers with their gals make love on the dry cane pile. I can hear it rattle.

"I have come out of the big house, me and my bottle, and I creep along, low on the ground, 'til I get up close. There I lie. I'm a little drunk. It all makes me happy. I can sleep some, on the ground like that, when the niggers are singing, when no one knows I'm there.

"I could sleep here, on these bricks here," David said, pointing to where the shadows cast by the broad leaves of the banana plants were broadest and deepest.

He got up from his chair and went limping, dragging one foot after the other, across the patio and lay down on the bricks.

For a long time Aunt Sally and I sat looking at each other, saying nothing, and presently she made a sign with her fat finger and we crept away into the house. "I'll let you out at the front door. You let him sleep, right where he is," she said. In spite of her huge bulk and her age she walked across the patio floor as softly as a kitten. Beside her I felt awkward and uncertain. When we had got inside she whispered to me. She had some champagne left from the old days, hidden away somewhere in the old house. "I'm going to send a magnum up to his dad when he goes home," she explained.

She, it seemed, was very happy, having him there, drunk and asleep on the brick floor of the patio. "We used to have some good men come here in the old days too," she said. As we went into the house through the kitchen door I had looked back at David, asleep now in the heavy shadows at a corner of the wall. There was no doubt he also was happy, had been happy ever since I had brought him into the presence of Aunt Sally. What a small huddled figure of a man he looked, lying thus on the brick, under the night sky, in the deep shadows of the banana plants.

I went into the house and out at the front door and into a dark narrow street, thinking. Well, I was, after all, a Northern man. It was possible Aunt Sally had become completely Southern, being down here so long.

I remembered that it was the chief boast of her life that once she had shaken hands with John L. Sullivan and that she had known P. T. Barnum.

"I knew Dave Gears. You mean to tell me you don't know who Dave Gears was? Why, he was one of the biggest gamblers we ever had in this city."

As for David and his poetry—it is in the manner of Shelley. "If I could write like Shelley I would be happy. I wouldn't care what happened to me," he had said during our walk of the early part of the evening.

I went along enjoying my thoughts. The street was dark and occasionally I laughed. A notion had come to me. It kept dancing in my head and I thought it very delicious. It had something to do with aristocrats, with such people as Aunt Sally and David. "Lordy," I thought, "maybe I do understand them a little. I'm from the Middle West myself and it seems we can produce our aristocrats too." I kept thinking of Aunt Sally and of my native State,

Ohio. "Lordy, I hope she comes from up there, but I don't think I had better inquire too closely into her past," I said to myself, as I went smiling away into the soft smoky night.

THE FLOOD

THE FLOOD

I T came about while he was trying to do a very difficult thing. He was a college professor and was trying to write a book on the subject of values.

A good many men had written on the subject, but now he was trying his hand.

He had read, he said, everything he could find that had been written on the subject.

There had been books consumed, months spent sitting and reading books.

The man had a house of his own at the edge of the town where stood the college in which he taught, but he was not teaching that year. It was his sabbatical year. There was a whole year to be spent just on his book.

"I thought," he said, "I would go to Europe." He thought of some quiet place, say in a little Normandy town. He remembered such a town he had once visited.

It would have to be very quiet, a place where no one would know him, where he would be undisturbed.

He had got a world of notes down into little books, piled neatly on a long work table in his room. He was a small alert almost bald man and had been married, but his wife was dead. He told me that for years he had been a very lonely man.

He had lived alone in his house for several years, having no children. There was an old housekeeper. There was a walled garden.

The old housekeeper did not sleep in the house. She came there early in the morning and went to her own home at night.

Nothing had happened to the man for months at a time, through several years, he said.

He had been lonely, had felt his loneliness a good deal. He hadn't much of a way with people.

He had, I gathered, before that Summer, been rather hungry for people. "My wife was a cheerful soul, when she was here," he said, speaking of his loneliness. I got from him and others—I had never known his wife—the sense of her as a rather frivolous-seeming woman.

She had been a light-hearted little woman, fond of frills, one of the kind whose blond hair is always flying in the wind. They are always chattering, that kind. They love everyone. My friend, the scholar, had adored his wife.

And then she had died, and there he was. He

was one of the sort who hurry along through streets, with books under their arms. You are always seeing such men about college towns. They go along staring at people with their impersonal eyes. If you speak to such a one he answers you absent-mindedly. "Don't bother me, please," he seems to be saying, while all the time, within himself, he is cursing himself that he cannot be more outgoing toward people.

He told me that, when his wife was alive and he was in his study, absorbed in his books, taking notes, lost in thought as one might say, preparing to write his book on values that was to be his magnum opus, she used to come in there.

She would come in, put one arm about his neck, lean over him, kiss him, and with the other hand would punch him in the stomach.

He said she used to drag him out and make him play croquet on the lawn or help with the garden. It was her money, he said, that had built the house.

He said she always called him an old stick.

"Come on, you old stick, kiss me, make love to me," she said to him sometimes. "You aren't much good to me or anyone, but you're all I've got." She would have people in, worlds of people, just anyone. When the house was full of people and the scholar, that little wide-eyed man, was standing about among them, rather confused, trying, in the midst of the hubbub, to hang onto his thoughts on the subject of values, remembering the far dim reaches of thought that occasionally came to him when he was alone . . . In him a feeling that all of man's notions of values, particularly in America, had got distorted, "perverted," he said, and that, when he was alone, when his wife and the people she was always dragging into the house did not disturb him—he had a feeling sometimes, at moments, when he was undisturbed thus, that persistent mind of his reaching out, himself impersonal, untouched . . . "I almost thought sometimes," he said, "that I had got something."

"There was," he said, "a kind of divine balance to all values to be found."

You got, to be sure, the crude sense of values that every one understands, values in land, money, possessions.

Then you got more subtle values, feeling coming in.

You got a painting, let us say by Rembrandt, selling to a rich man for fifty thousand dollars.

That is enough money to raise a dozen poor families, add some fifty or sixty citizens to the State.

The citizens being, let us say, all worthy men and women, without question of value to the State, producers, let us say.

Then you got the Rembrandt painting, hanging on a wall, say in some rich man's house, he having people into his house. He would stand before the painting.

He would brag about it as though he had himself painted it.

"I was pretty shrewd to get it at all," he would say. He would tell how he got it. Another rich man had been after it.

He talked about it as he might have talked about getting control of some industry by a skillful maneuver in the stock market.

Just the same it, the painting, was, in some way, adding a kind of value to that rich man's life.

It, the painting, was hanging on his wall, producing by hanging there nothing he could put his fingers on, producing no food, no clothes, nothing at all in the material world.

He himself being essentially a man of the material world. He had got rich being that.

Just the same . . .

My acquaintance, the scholar, wanted to be very just. No, that wasn't it. He said he wanted truth.

His mind reached out. He got hold of things a

little sometimes, or thought he did. He took notes,
he prepared to write his book.

He adored his wife and sometimes, often, he said
he hated her. She used to laugh at him. "Your old
values," she said. It seems he had been on that subject for years. He used to read papers before philo-
sophical societies and afterward they were printed
in little pamphlets by the societies. No one understood them, not even perhaps his fellow-philoso-
phers, but he read them aloud to his wife.

"Kiss me, kiss me hard," she would say. "Do it
now. Don't wait."

He wanted to kill her sometimes, he said. He
said he adored her.

She died. He was alone. He was bitterly lonely
sometimes.

People, remembering his wife, came for a time
to see him, but he was cold with them. It was because he was absorbed in thought. They talked to
him and he replied absent-mindedly. "Yes, that's so.
Perhaps you're right." Remarks of that kind.

Wanting them just the same, he said.

Then, he said, the flood came. He said **you**
couldn't account for floods.

"What's the use talking of balance?" he asked. "There is no balance."

He couldn't account for what happened during the Summer of that sabbatical year. He had a theory about life. I had heard it before.

"Everything in life comes in surges, floods, really. There is a whole city, thousands, even millions of people in it," he said.

"They are all, let us say, dull; they are all stupid; they are coarse and crude.

"All of them have become bored with life; they are full of hatreds for each other.

"It is not only cities. Whole nations are like that sometimes.

"How else are you to account for wars?

"And then there are other times when whole neighborhoods, whole cities, whole nations become something else. They are all irreligious, and then suddenly, without any cause any one has ever understood, ever perhaps can understand, they become religious. They are proud and they become humble, full of hatred and then suddenly filled with love.

"The individual, trying to assert himself against the mass, always without success, is drowned in a flood.

"There is a lifetime of work and thought washed away thus.

"There are these little tragedies. Are they tragedies or are they merely amusing?"

He, my friend the scholar, was seeking, as I have said, a kind of impersonal delicate balance on the subject of values.

That, in solitude, to be transcribed into words. His book, that was to be his magnum opus, the work of a lifetime justified.

There was no wife to bother him now by dragging people into the house.

There was no wife to say, "Come on, old stick, kiss me quick, now, while I want your kisses.

"Get this, get what I have to offer you while I have it to offer."

That sort of thing, of course, pitching him down off his mountain top of thought, thump.

He having to struggle for days afterwards, trying to get back up there again.

In his thinking he had, alone that Summer in his house, almost achieved the thing, the perfect balance of thought.

He said he struggled all through the Winter, Spring and early Summer. For years no one had come to see him.

Then suddenly his wife's sister, a younger sister, came. She hadn't even written him for a year, and then she telegraphed she was coming that way. It seems she was driving in a car, going to some place; he couldn't remember where.

She brought a young woman, a cousin, with her. The cousin, like his wife's sister, was another frivolous one.

And then the scholar's brother came. He was a big boastful youngish man who was in business.

He only came to stay a day or two, but, like the scholar, he had lost his wife. He was attracted to the two young women.

He stayed on and on because of them. They may have stayed on and on because of him.

He was a man who had a big car. He brought other men into the house.

Suddenly the scholar's house was filled with men and women. There was a good deal of gin-drinking.

There was a flood of people. The scholar's brother brought in a phonograph and wanted to install a radio.

There were dances in the evening.

Even the old housekeeper caught it. She had always been rather quiet, a staid, sad old woman. One evening the scholar said, after a day, during the afternoon of which he had struggled and struggled, alone in his room, the door shut, sound coming in nevertheless, coarse sounds, he said, sound of women's laughter, men's voices.

He said the two young women who had come there and who he believed had stayed because of his brother—he having stayed because of them—the two had met other people of the town. They filled his house with people.

He had, however, almost got something he was after in spite of them.

"I swear I almost had it."

"Had what?"

"Why, my definition of values. There had to be something, you see, at the very core of my book."

"Yes, of course."

"I mean one place in my book where everything was defined. In simple words, so that everyone could understand."

"Of course."

I shall never forget the scholar when he was telling me all this, the puzzled, half-hurt, look in his eyes.

He said they had even got his housekeeper going. "What do you think of it—she also drinking gin?"

There was a crash of sounds that afternoon in his house.

He was alone in his room upstairs in his house, in his study.

They had got the sad, staid old housekeeper going. He said his brother was very efficient. They had her dancing to the music of the phonograph. The scholar's brother, that big blustering bragging man—he was a manufacturer of some sort—was dancing with the housekeeper—with that staid, sad old woman.

The others had got into a circle.

The phonograph was going.

What happened was that the scholar's sister—just, I imagine from all he said and from what others afterward said of her, a miniature edition, a new printing one might say, of his dead wife . . .

She, it seems, came running upstairs and burst into his room, her blond hair flying. She was laughing.

"I had almost got it," he said.

"What? Oh, yes. Your definition."

"Yes, just the definition I had been after for years."

"I was about to write it down. It embraced all, everything I had to say."

She burst in.

I gather the sister must have been at least a little in love with the man and that he, after all, did not want the bragging, blustering brother to have her. He admitted that.

She rushed in.

"Come on, you old stick," she said to him.

He said he tried to explain to her. "I made a fight," he said.

He got up from his desk and tried to reason with her. She had fairly taken possession of his house.

He tried to tell her what he was up to. He spoke of standing there, beside his desk, where he sat when he told me all this, trying to explain all this to her.

I thought the scholar got a bit vulgar when he told me of that moment.

"There was nothing doing," he said. He had got that expression from the young woman, his wife's sister.

She was laughing at him as his wife had formerly done; she wouldn't have kissed him.

She wouldn't have said, "Kiss me quick, you old stick, while I feel that way."

I gathered she merely dragged him downstairs. He said he went with her, couldn't help himself, couldn't, of course, be rude to her, his wife's sister.

He went with her and saw his staid, sad old housekeeper acting like that.

The housekeeper didn't seem to care whether he saw or not. She had broken loose. The whole house had broken loose.

And so, in the end, my acquaintance, the scholar, didn't care either.

"I was in the flood," he said. "What was the use?"

He was a little afraid that, if he didn't do something about it, his bragging brother, or some man like him, might get his wife's sister.

He didn't quite want that to happen. So that evening, when he was alone with her, he proposed to her.

He said she called him an old stick. "It must have been a family expression," he said. Something of the scholar came back into him when he said that.

He had been caught in a flood. He had let go.

He had proposed to his wife's sister, in the garden back of his house, under an apple tree, near the croquet grounds, and she had said . . .

He didn't tell me what she said. I imagine she said, "Yes, you old stick."

"Kiss me quick while I feel that way," she said.

That, at least, gets a certain balance to my tale.

The scholar; however, says there is no balance. "There are only floods, one flood following another," he says. When I talked to him of all this he was a bit discouraged.

However, he seemed cheerful enough.

WHY THEY GOT MARRIED

WHY THEY GOT MARRIED

PEOPLE keep on getting married. Evidently hope is eternal in the human breast. Every one laughs about it. You cannot go to a show but that some comedian takes a shot at the institution of marriage —and gets a laugh. It is amusing to watch the faces of married couples at such moments.

But I had intended to speak about Will. Will is a painter. I had intended to tell you about a conversation that took place in Will's apartment one night. Every man or woman who marries must wonder sometimes how it happened to be just that other one he or she married.

"You have to live so close to the other when you are married," said Will.

"Yes, you do," said Helen, his wife.

"I get awfully tired of it sometimes," Will said.

"And don't I?" said Helen.

"It is worse for me than it is for you."

"No, I think it is worse for me."

"Well, gracious sakes, I would like to know how you figure that out."

"I was in New York, was a student there," said Will. It was evident that he had risen above the little choppy matrimonial sea in which he had been swimming with Helen—conversational swimming—he was ready to tell how it happened. That is always an interesting moment.

"Well," said Will, "as I said, there I was, in New York. I was a young bachelor. I was going to school. Then I got through school. I got a job. It wasn't much of a job. I got thirty dollars a week. I was making advertising drawings. So I met a fellow named Bob. He was getting his seventy-five dollars a week. Think of that, Helen. Why didn't you get that one?"

"But, Will, dear, you are now making more than he will ever make," Helen said. "But it wasn't only that. Will is such a sweet, gentle man. You can see that by just looking at him." She walked across the room and took her husband's hands.

"You can't tell about that gentle-looking kind sometimes," I said.

"I know it," Helen said, smiling.

She was surely a very lovely thing at that moment. She had big gray eyes and was very slender and graceful.

260

Will said that the man Bob, he had met, had some relatives living over near Philadelphia. He was, Helen said, a large, rather mushy-looking man with white hands.

So they began going over there for week-ends. Will and Bob. Will's own people lived in Kansas.

At the place where Bob had the relatives—it was in a suburb of Philadelphia—there were two girls. They were cousins of Bob's.

Will said the girls were all right, and when he said it Helen smiled. He said their father was an advertising man. "They made us welcome at their house. They gave us grand beds to sleep in." Will had got launched into his tale.

"We would get over there about five o'clock of a Saturday afternoon. The father's name was J. G. Small. He had a swell-looking car.

"So he would be at home and he would take a look at us, the way an older man does look at two young fellows making up to the young women folks in his house. At first he looks at you as much as to say, 'Hello, I envy you your youth, etc.,' and then he takes another look and his eyes say, 'What are you hanging around here for, you young squirt?'

"After dinner, of a Saturday night, we got the car, or rather the girls did. I sat on the back seat with one of them. Her name was Cynthia.

"She was a tall, heavy-looking girl with dark eyes. She embarrassed me. I don't know why."

Will went a bit aside from his subject to speak of men's embarrassment with such women. "There is a certain kind that just get your goat," he said, speaking a bit inelegantly, I thought, for a painter. "They feel they ought to be up to their business, getting themselves a man, but maybe they have thought too much about it. They are self-conscious and, of course, they make you feel that way.

"Naturally, we made love. It seemed to be expected. Bob was at it with her sister on the front seat. Everybody does it nowadays, and I was glad enough for the chance. Just the same I kept wishing it came a little more natural with me—with that one I mean."

When Will was saying all this to me he was sitting on a couch in his apartment in New York. I had dined with him and his wife. She was sitting on the couch beside him. When he spoke about the other woman, she crept a little nearer to him. She remarked casually that it was only a chance that she, instead of the woman Cynthia, got Will. When she said that, it was very hard to believe her. I doubt whether she wanted me to believe.

Will said that, with Cynthia, it was very hard indeed to get close. He said she never really did, what he called "melt." The fellow on the front seat, that is to say his friend Bob, was usually in a playful mood during these drives. Of the two girls, his cousins, he always seemed to prefer, not the one named Cynthia, but a smaller, darker, livelier one named Grace. He used to stop the car sometimes, on a dark road in that country somewhere outside Philadelphia, and he and Grace would make up to each other.

It was simply amazing how the girl named Grace could talk. Will said she used to swear at Bob and that when he got, what she called "too gay," she hit him. Sometimes Bob stopped the car and he and Grace got out and took a walk. They would be gone quite a long time. Will sat in the back seat with Cynthia. He said her hands were like men's hands. "They looked like competent hands," he thought. She was older than her sister Grace, and had taken a job in the city.

Apparently she was not very competent in love making; Will thought Grace and Bob would never come back. He was trying to think up things to say to Cynthia. One night they all went together to a dance. It was at a road-house, somewhere near Philadelphia.

It must have been a rather tough place. Will said it was, but when he said so, his wife, Helen, laughed. "What the devil were you doing there any-way?" Will suddenly said, turning and glaring at her as though it were the first time he had thought of asking the question.

"I was after a man and I got one, too. I got you," she said.

She had gone to the dance with a young man of the same suburb in which Bob's cousins lived. Her father was a doctor. Helen took the tale right out of Will's hands. She explained that when Will and Bob and the two girls, Grace and Cynthia, came into the dance hall she spotted Will at once. "That one's mine," she said to herself and almost before they had got inside the door she had been introduced to Will. They danced together at once.

There must really have been some tough people in the road-house that night. When Will and Helen were dancing together there was a big, low-browed, tough-looking fellow who kept trying to "make" Helen, Will said. He had started to tell me about it and then got an idea. "Say, you look here, Helen," he said, turning to look at his wife, "didn't you have something to do with that? Had you given that low-browed man the eye? Were you egging him on?"

"Sure," she said.

She explained that when a woman, like herself, was at work, when she really was laying herself out to get a man, the right thing to do was to have a rival in the field. "You have to work with what material you have at hand, don't you? You are an artist. You are always talking about art. You ought to understand that."

There came very near being a row. Will had taken Helen to a table where Bob sat with Grace and Cynthia. The young tough swaggered up—he was a little high—and demanded a dance with Helen.

Helen got indignant. She looked frightened and Will felt it was up to him, and he isn't the kind that is good at that sort of thing. Will is the kind that in such an emergency grows rather helpless.

Such a man begins to tremble. His back hurts. He dreams of being cool and determined, but is so helpless that very likely he shouts, makes the situation much worse, goes too far. What happened was that Helen settled the matter. She had already become a little tender about Will.

"What did you do?" I asked. "I understood you had become indignant."

"I had," she said, "but I managed. I got up and danced with him. I liked it. He was a good dancer."

Helen, like Grace and Cynthia, had got her father's car for the evening. When they left that tough place the young man who had come with her was on the back seat of the other car with Cynthia, and Will was in the car with her. That did not much please Cynthia, but it seemed Cynthia had very little to do with it.

So they had got started in that way. Afterward, Will continued going to Philadelphia with Bob for the week-ends, but things were different at the cousin's house. "It was not so warm and cheerful there," Will said. Helen was always dropping in. Soon the two young men began stopping at a hotel in Philadelphia. Bob had also got interested in Helen. They stopped at a cheap hotel, not having much money, and Helen came to see them. Will said she came right up into the hotel bedroom. As he began thinking of what went on during that time, Will looked at Helen with a kind of wonder in his eyes. "I guess you could have had either of us," he said, with a note of awe in his voice. It was obvious he admired his wife.

"I was not so sure about Bob," Helen said.

She wrote letters to both of the men during the week, when they were in New York at work, and when they arrived in Philadelphia, there she was. She always managed to get her father's car. She went home to her suburb late on Saturday nights and came back again early on Sundays. Saturday nights they all went together to a dance.

One day her father grew alarmed and angry, and followed her. He saw her go to the two men, right into their room, in the cheap hotel.

She had to decide the matter. She had made up her mind to marry one of the men, was tired of living at home. Things, I gathered, were getting rather warm at home. She was an only child. She said her mother was crying all the time and her father was furious. "I had to be hard-boiled with them for the time," she explained. She was rather like a surgeon about to perform an operation on a frightened patient. She cajoled and bullied them. When her father tried to put his foot down she issued an ultimatum. "I'm twenty-one," she said. "If you interfere with me I shall leave home."

"But how will you live?"

"Don't be silly, Father, a woman can always live."

She went right out to the garage, got her father's car and drove to Philadelphia. In the room in the hotel she was studying the two men. She got Will to go down to the car with her. "Get in," she said. They drove away from the hotel. "I didn't know where we were going," Will said.

They drove and drove. Will spoke of her mood

that night. He was in love. When I heard this tale he was still very much in love. "It was a soft clear night with stars." Speaking of it, he took hold of his wife's hands.

"Let's get married," she said to Will that night. "But when?" he asked. She thought they had better do it at once. "But think of my salary," Will said. "I am thinking about it. It isn't much, is it?" The meagerness of his salary didn't seem to alter her determination. "I can't wait any longer," was what she said. She said they would drive around all night and get married early the next morning.

And so they did. Her people, the doctor and his wife, were in a panic.

Will and his wife went to them the next day. "How were you received?" I asked. "Fine," Will said. He said that the doctor and his wife would have been happy no matter whom she had married. "You see, I had arranged for that," Helen said. "I had got them into a state where marriage sure seemed like salvation to them."

BROTHER DEATH

BROTHER DEATH

THERE were the two oak stumps, knee high to a
not-too-tall man and cut quite squarely across. They
became to the two children objects of wonder.
They had seen the two trees cut but had run away
just as the trees fell. They hadn't thought of the
two stumps, to be left standing there; hadn't even
looked at them. Afterwards Ted said to his sister
Mary, speaking of the stumps: "I wonder if they
bled, like legs, when a surgeon cuts a man's leg off."
He had been hearing war stories. A man came to the
farm one day to visit one of the farm-hands, a man
who had been in the World War and had lost an
arm. He stood in one of the barns talking. When
Ted said that Mary spoke up at once. She hadn't
been lucky enough to be at the barn when the one-
armed man was there talking, and was jealous. "Why
not a woman or a girl's leg?" she said, but Ted said
the idea was silly. "Women and girls don't get their
legs and arms cut off," he declared. "Why not? I'd
just like to know why not?" Mary kept saying.

It would have been something if they had stayed,

that day the trees were cut. "We might have gone and touched the places," Ted said. He meant the stumps. Would they have been warm? Would they have bled? They did go and touch the places afterwards, but it was a cold day and the stumps were cold. Ted stuck to his point that only men's arms and legs were cut off, but Mary thought of automobile accidents. "You can't think just about wars. There might be an automobile accident," she declared, but Ted wouldn't be convinced.

They were both children, but something had made them both in an odd way old. Mary was fourteen and Ted eleven, but Ted wasn't strong and that rather evened things up. They were the children of a well-to-do Virginia farmer named John Grey in the Blue Ridge country in Southwestern Virginia. There was a wide valley called the "Rich Valley," with a railroad and a small river running through it and high mountains in sight, to the north and south. Ted had some kind of heart disease, a lesion, something of the sort, the result of a severe attack of diphtheria when he was a child of eight. He was thin and not strong but curiously alive. The doctor said he might die at any moment, might just drop down dead. The fact had drawn him peculiarly close to his sister Mary. It had awakened a strong and determined maternalism in her.

The whole family, the neighbors, on neighboring farms in the valley, and even the other children at the schoolhouse where they went to school recognized something as existing between the two children. "Look at them going along there," people said. "They do seem to have good times together, but they are so serious. For such young children they are too serious. Still, I suppose, under the circumstances, it's natural." Of course, everyone knew about Ted. It had done something to Mary. At fourteen she was both a child and a grown woman. The woman side of her kept popping out at unexpected moments.

She had sensed something concerning her brother Ted. It was because he was as he was, having that kind of a heart, a heart likely at any moment to stop beating, leaving him dead, cut down like a young tree. The others in the Grey family, that is to say, the older ones, the mother and father and an older brother, Don, who was eighteen now, recognized something as belonging to the two children, being, as it were, between them, but the recognition wasn't very definite. People in your own family are likely at any moment to do strange, sometimes hurtful things to you. You have to watch them. Ted and Mary had both found that out.

The brother Don was like the father, already

at eighteen almost a grown man. He was that sort, the kind people speak of, saying: "He's a good man. He'll make a good solid dependable man." The father, when he was a young man, never drank, never went chasing the girls, was never wild. There had been enough wild young ones in the Rich Valley when he was a lad. Some of them had inherited big farms and had lost them, gambling, drinking, fooling with fast horses and chasing after the women. It had been almost a Virginia tradition, but John Grey was a land man. All the Greys were. There were other large cattle farms owned by Greys up and down the valley.

John Grey, every one said, was a natural cattle man. He knew beef cattle, of the big so-called export type, how to pick and feed them to make beef. He knew how and where to get the right kind of young stock to turn into his fields. It was blue-grass country. Big beef cattle went directly off the pastures to market. The Grey farm contained over twelve hundred acres, most of it in blue grass.

The father was a land man, land hungry. He had begun, as a cattle farmer, with a small place, inherited from his father, some two hundred acres, lying next to what was then the big Aspinwahl place and, after he began, he never stopped getting more land. He kept cutting in on the Aspinwahls who were a rather horsey, fast lot. They thought of themselves as Virginia aristocrats, having, as they weren't so modest about pointing out, a family going back and back, family tradition, guests always being entertained, fast horses kept, money being bet on fast horses. John Grey getting their land, now twenty acres, then thirty, then fifty, until at last he got the old Aspinwahl house, with one of the Aspinwahl girls, not a young one, not one of the best-looking ones, as wife. The Aspinwahl place was down, by that time, to less than a hundred acres, but he went on, year after year, always being careful and shrewd, making every penny count, never wasting a cent, adding and adding to what was now the Grey place. The former Aspinwahl house was a large old brick house with fireplaces in all the rooms and was very comfortable.

People wondered why Louise Aspinwahl had married John Grey, but when they were wondering they smiled. The Aspinwahl girls were all well educated, had all been away to college, but Louise wasn't so pretty. She got nicer after marriage, suddenly almost beautiful. The Aspinwahls were, as every one knew, naturally sensitive, really first class but the men couldn't hang onto land and the Greys could. In all that section of Virginia, people gave John Grey credit for being what he was. They respected him. "He's on the level," they said, "as honest as a horse. He has cattle sense, that's it." He could run his big hand down over the flank of a steer and say, almost to the pound, what he would weigh on the scales or he could look at a calf or a yearling and say, "He'll do," and he would do. A steer is a steer. He isn't supposed to do anything but make beef.

There was Don, the oldest son of the Grey family. He was so evidently destined to be a Grey, to be another like his father. He had long been a star in the 4H Club of the Virginia county and, even as a lad of nine and ten, had won prizes at steer judging. At twelve he had produced, no one helping him, doing all the work himself, more bushels of corn on an acre of land than any other boy in the State.

It was all a little amazing, even a bit queer to Mary Grey, being as she was a girl peculiarly conscious, so old and young, so aware. There was Don, the older brother, big and strong of body, like the father, and there was the young brother Ted. Ordinarily, in the ordinary course of life, she being what she was—female—it would have been quite natural and right for her to have given her young girl's admiration to Don but she didn't. For some reason, Don barely existed for her. He was outside, not in it, while for her Ted, the seemingly weak one of the family, was everything.

Still there Don was, so big of body, so quiet, so apparently sure of himself. The father had begun, as a young cattle man, with the two hundred acres, and now he had the twelve hundred. What would Don Grey do when he started? Already he knew, although he didn't say anything, that he wanted to start. He wanted to run things, be his own boss. His father had offered to send him away to college, to an agricultural college, but he wouldn't go. "No. I can learn more here," he said.

Already there was a contest, always kept under the surface, between the father and son. It concerned ways of doing things, decisions to be made. As yet the son always surrendered.

It is like that in a family, little isolated groups formed within the larger group, jealousies, concealed hatreds, silent battles secretly going on— among the Greys, Mary and Ted, Don and his father, the mother and the two younger children, Gladys, a girl child of six now, who adored her brother Don, and Harry, a boy child of two.

As for Mary and Ted, they lived within their own world, but their own world had not been established without a struggle. The point was that Ted, having the heart that might at any moment stop beating, was always being treated tenderly by the others. Only Mary understood that—how it infuriated and hurt him.

"No, Ted, I wouldn't do that."

"Now, Ted, do be careful."

Sometimes Ted went white and trembling with anger, Don, the father, the mother, all keeping at him like that. It didn't matter what he wanted to do, learn to drive one of the two family cars, climb a tree to find a bird's nest, run a race with Mary. Naturally, being on a farm, he wanted to try his hand at breaking a colt, beginning with him, getting a saddle on, having it out with him. "No, Ted. You can't." He had learned to swear, picking it up from the farm-hands and from boys at the country school. "Hell! Goddam!" he said to Mary. Only Mary understood how he felt, and she had not put the matter very definitely into words, not even to herself. It was one of the things that made her old when she was so young. It made her stand aside from the others of the family, aroused in her a curious determination. "They shall not." She caught herself saying the words to herself. "They shall not.

"If he is to have but a few years of life, they shall not spoil what he is to have. Why should they make him die, over and over, day after day?" The thoughts in her did not become so definite. She had resentment against the others. She was like a soldier, standing guard over Ted.

The two children drew more and more away, into their own world and only once did what Mary felt come to the surface. That was with the mother.

It was on an early Summer day and Ted and Mary were playing in the rain. They were on a side porch of the house, where the water came pouring down from the eaves. At a corner of the porch there was a great stream, and first Ted and then Mary dashed through it, returning to the porch with clothes soaked and water running in streams from soaked hair. There was something joyous, the feel of the cold water on the body, under clothes, and they were shrieking with laugher when the mother came to the door. She looked at Ted. There was fear and anxiety in her voice. "Oh, Ted, you know you mustn't, you mustn't." Just that. All the rest implied. Nothing said to Mary. There it was. "Oh, Ted, you mustn't. You mustn't run hard, climb trees, ride horses. The least shock to you may do it." It was the old story again, and, of course, Ted understood. He went white and trembled. Why couldn't the rest understand that was a hundred times worse for him? On that day, without answering his mother, he ran off the porch and through the rain toward the barns. He wanted to go hide himself from every one. Mary knew how he felt.

She got suddenly very old and very angry. The mother and daughter stood looking at each other, the woman nearing fifty and the child of fourteen. It was getting everything in the family reversed. Mary felt that but felt she had to do something. "You should have more sense, Mother," she said seriously. She also had gone white. Her lips trembled. "You mustn't do it any more. Don't you ever do it again."

"What, child?" There was astonishment and half anger in the mother's voice. "Always making him think of it," Mary said. She wanted to cry but didn't.

The mother understood. There was a queer tense moment before Mary also walked off, toward the barns, in the rain. It wasn't all so clear. The mother wanted to fly at the child, perhaps shake her for daring to be so impudent. A child like that to decide things—to dare to reprove her mother. There was so much implied—even that Ted be allowed to die, quickly, suddenly, rather than that death, danger of sudden death, be brought again and again to his attention. There were values in life, implied by a child's words: "Life, what is it worth? Is death the most terrible thing?" The mother turned and went silently into the house while Mary, going to the barns, presently found Ted. He was in an empty horse stall, standing with his back to the wall, staring. There were no explanations. "Well," Ted said presently, and, "Come on, Ted," Mary replied. It was necessary to do something, even perhaps more risky than playing in the rain. The rain was already passing. "Let's take off our shoes," Mary said. Going barefoot was one of the things forbidden Ted. They took their shoes off and, leaving them in the barn, went into an orchard. There was a small creek below the orchard, a creek that went down to the river and now it would be in flood. They went into it and once Mary got swept off her feet so that Ted had to pull her out. She spoke then. "I told Mother," she said, looking serious.

"What?" Ted said. "Gee, I guess maybe I saved you from drowning," he added.

"Sure you did," said Mary. "I told her to let you alone." She grew suddenly fierce. "They've all got to—they've got to let you alone," she said.

There was a bond. Ted did his share. He was imaginative and could think of plenty of risky things to do. Perhaps the mother spoke to the father and to Don, the older brother. There was a new inclination in the family to keep hands off the pair, and the fact seemed to give the two children new room in life. Something seemed to open out. There was a little inner world created, always, every day, being re-created, and in it there was a kind of new security. It seemed to the two children—they could not have put their feeling into words—that, being in their own created world, feeling a new security there, they could suddenly look out at the outside world and see, in a new way, what was going on out there in the world that belonged also to others.

It was a world to be thought about, looked at, a world of drama too, the drama of human relations, outside their own world, in a family, on a farm, in a farmhouse.... On a farm, calves and yearling steers arriving to be fattened, great heavy steers going off to market, colts being broken to work or to saddle, lambs born in the late Winter. The human side of life was more difficult, to a child often incomprehensible, but after the speech to the mother, on the porch of the house that day when it rained, it seemed to Mary almost as though she and Ted had set up a new family. Everything about the farm, the house and the barns got nicer. There was a new freedom. The two children walked along a country road, returning to the farm from school in the late afternoon. There were other children in the road but they managed to fall behind or they got ahead. There were plans made. "I'm going to be a nurse

when I grow up," Mary said. She may have remembered dimly the woman nurse, from the county-seat
town, who had come to stay in the house when Ted
was so ill. Ted said that as soon as he could—it would
be when he was younger yet than Don was now—he
intended to leave and go out West . . . far out, he
said. He wanted to be a cowboy or a bronco-buster
or something, and, that failing, he thought he would
be a railroad engineer. The railroad that went down
through the Rich Valley crossed a corner of the
Grey farm, and, from the road in the afternoon, they
could sometimes see trains, quite far away, the smoke
rolling up. There was a faint rumbling noise, and,
on clear days they could see the flying piston rods
of the engines.

As for the two stumps in the field near the
house, they were what was left of two oak trees.
The children had known the trees. They were cut
one day in the early Fall.

There was a back porch to the Grey house—the
house that had once been the seat of the Aspinwahl
family—and from the porch steps a path led down to
a stone spring house. A spring came out of the
ground just there, and there was a tiny stream that
went along the edge of a field, past two large barns

and out across a meadow to a creek—called a "branch" in Virginia, and the two trees stood close together beyond the spring house and the fence.

They were lusty trees, their roots down in the rich, always damp soil, and one of them had a great limb that came down near the ground, so that Ted and Mary could climb into it and out another limb into its brother tree, and in the Fall, when other trees, at the front and side of the house, had shed their leaves, blood-red leaves still clung to the two oaks. They were like dry blood on gray days, but on other days, when the sun came out, the trees flamed against distant hills. The leaves clung, whispering and talking when the wind blew, so that the trees themselves seemed carrying on a conversation.

John Grey had decided he would have the trees cut. At first it was not a very definite decision. "I think I'll have them cut," he announced.

"But why?" his wife asked. The trees meant a good deal to her. They had been planted, just in that spot, by her grandfather, she said, having in mind just a certain effect. "You see how, in the Fall, when you stand on the back porch, they are so nice against the hills." She spoke of the trees, already quite large, having been brought from a distant woods. Her mother had often spoken of it. The man, her grandfather, had a special feeling for trees. "An

Aspinwahl would do that," John Grey said. "There is enough yard, here about the house, and enough trees. They do not shade the house or the yard. An Aspinwahl would go to all that trouble for trees and then plant them where grass might be growing." He had suddenly determined, a half-formed determination in him suddenly hardening. He had perhaps heard too much of the Aspinwahls and their ways. The conversation regarding the trees took place at the table, at the noon hour, and Mary and Ted heard it all.

It began at the table and was carried on afterwards out of doors, in the yard back of the house. The wife had followed her husband out. He always left the table suddenly and silently, getting quickly up and going out heavily, shutting doors with a bang as he went. "Don't, John," the wife said, standing on the porch and calling to her husband. It was a cold day but the sun was out and the trees were like great bonfires against gray distant fields and hills. The older son of the family, young Don, the one so physically like the father and apparently so like him in every way, had come out of the house with the mother, followed by the two children, Ted and Mary, and at first Don said nothing, but, when the father did not answer the mother's protest but started toward the barn, he also spoke. What he said was obviously the determining thing, hardening the father.

To the two other children—they had walked a little aside and stood together watching and listening—there was something. There was their own child's world. "Let us alone and we'll let you alone." It wasn't as definite as that. Most of the definite thoughts about what happened in the yard that afternoon came to Mary Grey long afterwards, when she was a grown woman. At the moment there was merely a sudden sharpening of the feeling of isolation, a wall between herself and Ted and the others. The father, even then perhaps, seen in a new light, Don and the mother seen in a new light.

There was something, a driving destructive thing in life, in all relationships between people. All of this felt dimly that day—she always believed both by herself and Ted—but only thought out long afterwards, after Ted was dead. There was the farm her father had won from the Aspinwahls—greater persistence, greater shrewdness. In a family, little remarks dropped from time to time, an impression slowly built up. The father, John Grey, was a successful man. He had acquired. He owned. He was the commander, the one having power to do his will. And the power had run out and covered, not only other human lives, impulses in others,

wishes, hungers in others ... he himself might not
have, might not even understand ... but it went far
out beyond that. It was, curiously, the power also
of life and death. Did Mary Grey think such
thoughts at that moment? ...? She couldn't have. ...
Still there was her own peculiar situation, her relationship with her brother Ted, who was to die.

Ownership that gave curious rights, dominances
—fathers over children, men and women over lands,
houses, factories in cities, fields. "I will have the
trees in that orchard cut. They produce apples but
not of the right sort. There is no money in apples
of that sort any more."

"But, Sir ... you see ... look ... the trees there
against that hill, against the sky."

"Nonsense. Sentimentality."

Confusion.

It would have been such nonsense to think of the
father of Mary Grey as a man without feeling. He
had struggled hard all his life, perhaps, as a young
man, gone without things wanted, deeply hungered
for. Some one has to manage things in this life. Possessions mean power, the right to say, "do this" or
"do that." If you struggle long and hard for a thing
it becomes infinitely sweet to you.

Was there a kind of hatred between the father
and the older son of the Grey family? "You are one

also who has this thing—the impulse to power, so like my own. Now you are young and I am growing old." Admiration mixed with fear. If you would retain power it will not do to admit fear.

The young Don was so curiously like the father. There were the same lines about the jaws, the same eyes. They were both heavy men. Already the young man walked like the father, slammed doors as did the father. There was the same curious lack of delicacy of thought and touch—the heaviness that plows through, gets things done. When John Grey had married Louise Aspinwahl he was already a mature man, on his way to success. Such men do not marry young and recklessly. Now he was nearing sixty and there was the son—so like himself, having the same kind of strength.

Both land lovers, possession lovers. "It is my farm, my house, my horses, cattle, sheep." Soon now, another ten years, fifteen at the most, and the father would be ready for death. "See, already my hand slips a little. All of this to go out of my grasp." He, John Grey, had not got all of these possessions so easily. It had taken much patience, much persistence. No one but himself would ever quite know. Five, ten, fifteen years of work and saving, getting the Aspinwahl farm piece by piece. "The fools!" They had liked to think of themselves as aristocrats, throwing the land away, now twenty acres, now thirty, now fifty.

Raising horses that could never plow an acre of land.

And they had robbed the land too, had never put anything back, doing nothing to enrich it, build it up. Such a one thinking: "I'm an Aspinwahl, a gentleman. I do not soil my hands at the plow.

"Fools who do not know the meaning of land owned, possessions, money—responsibility. It is they who are second-rate men."

He had got an Aspinwahl for a wife and, as it had turned out, she was the best, the smartest and, in the end, the best-looking one of the lot.

And now there was his son, standing at the moment near the mother. They had both come down off the porch. It would be natural and right for this one—he being what he already was, what he would become—for him, in his turn, to come into possession, to take command.

There would be, of course, the rights of the other children. If you have the stuff in you (John Grey felt that his son Don had) there is a way to manage. You buy the others out, make arrangements. There was Ted—he wouldn't be alive—and Mary and the two younger children. "The better for you if you have to struggle."

All of this, the implication of the moment of sudden struggle between a father and son, coming slowly afterwards to the man's daughter, as yet little more than a child. Does the drama take place when the seed is put into the ground or afterwards when the plant has pushed out of the ground and the bud breaks open, or still later, when the fruit ripens? There were the Greys with their ability—slow, saving, able, determined, patient. Why had they superseded the Aspinwahls in the Rich Valley? Aspinwahl blood also in the two children, Mary and Ted.

There was an Aspinwahl man—called "Uncle Fred," a brother to Louise Grey—who came sometimes to the farm. He was a rather striking-looking, tall old man with a gray Vandyke beard and a mustache, somewhat shabbily dressed but always with an indefinable air of class. He came from the county-seat town, where he lived now with a daughter who had married a merchant, a polite courtly old man who always froze into a queer silence in the presence of his sister's husband.

The son Don was standing near the mother on the day in the Fall, and the two children, Mary and Ted, stood apart.

"Don't, John," Louise Grey said again. The father, who had started away toward the barns, stopped.

"Well, I guess I will."

"No, you won't," said young Don, speaking suddenly. There was a queer fixed look in his eyes. It had flashed into life—something that was between the two men: "I possess". . ."I will possess." The father wheeled and looked sharply at the son and then ignored him.

For a moment the mother continued pleading. "But why, why?"

"They make too much shade. The grass does not grow."

"But there is so much grass, so many acres of grass."

John Grey was answering his wife, but now again he looked at his son. There were unspoken words flying back and forth.

"I possess. I am in command here. What do you mean by telling me that I won't?"

"Ha! So! You possess now but soon I will possess."

"I'll see you in hell first."

"You fool! Not yet! Not yet!"

None of the words, set down above, was spoken at the moment, and afterwards the daughter Mary never did remember the exact words that had passed between the two men. There was a sudden quick flash of determination in Don—even perhaps sudden determination to stand by the mother—even perhaps something else—a feeling in the young Don out of the Aspinwahl blood in him—for the moment tree love superseding grass love—grass that would fatten steers. . . .

Winner of 4H Club prizes, champion young corn-raiser, judge of steers, land lover, possession lover.

"You won't," Don said again.

"Won't what?"

"Won't cut those trees."

The father said nothing more at the moment but walked away from the little group toward the barns. The sun was still shining brightly. There was a sharp cold little wind. The two trees were like bonfires lighted against distant hills.

It was the noon hour and there were two men, both young, employees on the farm, who lived in a small tenant house beyond the barns. One of them, a man with a harelip, was married and the other, a rather handsome silent young man, boarded with him. They had just come from the midday meal and were going toward one of the barns. It was the beginning of the Fall corn-cutting time and they would be going together to a distant field to cut corn.

The father went to the barn and returned with the two men. They brought axes and a long cross-

cut saw. "I want you to cut those two trees." There
was something, a blind, even stupid determination
in the man, John Grey. And at that moment his
wife, the mother of his children ... There was no
way any of the children could ever know how many
moments of the sort she had been through. She had
married John Grey. He was her man.

"If you do, Father ..." Don Grey said coldly.

"Do as I tell you! Cut those two trees!" This
addressed to the two workmen. The one who had
a harelip laughed. His laughter was like the bray
of a donkey.

"Don't," said Louise Grey, but she was not
addressing her husband this time. She stepped to
her son and put a hand on his arm.

"Don't.

"Don't cross him. Don't cross my man." Could
a child like Mary Grey comprehend? It takes time
to understand things that happen in life. Life un-
folds slowly to the mind. Mary was standing with
Ted, whose young face was white and tense. Death
at his elbow. At any moment. At any moment.

"I have been through this a hundred times.
That is the way this man I married has succeeded.
Nothing stops him. I married him; I have had my
children by him.

"We women choose to submit.

"This is my affair, more than yours, Don, my son."

A woman hanging onto her thing—the family, created about her.

The son not seeing things with her eyes. He shook off his mother's hand, lying on his arm. Louise Grey was younger than her husband, but, if he was now nearing sixty, she was drawing near fifty. At the moment she looked very delicate and fragile. There was something, at the moment, in her bearing. . . . Was there, after all, something in blood, the Aspinwahl blood?

In a dim way perhaps, at the moment, the child Mary did comprehend. Women and their men. For her then, at that time, there was but one male, the child Ted. Afterwards she remembered how he looked at that moment, the curiously serious old look on his young face. There was even, she thought later, a kind of contempt for both the father and brother, as though he might have been saying to himself—he couldn't really have been saying it— he was too young: "Well, we'll see. This is something. These foolish ones—my father and my brother. I myself haven't long to live. I'll see what I can, while I do live."

The brother Don stepped over near to where his father stood.

"If you do, Father . . ." he said again.

"Well?"

"I'll walk off this farm and I'll never come back."

"All right. Go then."

The father began directing the two men who had begun cutting the trees, each man taking a tree. The young man with the harelip kept laughing, the laughter like the bray of a donkey. "Stop that," the father said sharply, and the sound ceased abruptly. The son Don walked away, going rather aimlessly toward the barn. He approached one of the barns and then stopped. The mother, white now, half ran into the house.

The son returned toward the house, passing the two younger children without looking at them, but did not enter. The father did not look at him. He went hesitatingly along a path at the front of the house and through a gate and into a road. The road ran for several miles down through the valley and then, turning, went over a mountain to the county-seat town.

As it happened, only Mary saw the son Don when he returned to the farm. There were three or four tense days. Perhaps, all the time, the mother and son had been secretly in touch. There was a telephone in the house. The father stayed all day in the fields, and when he was in the house was silent.

Mary was in one of the barns on the day when Don came back and when the father and son met. It was an odd meeting.

The son came, Mary always afterwards thought, rather sheepishly. The father came out of a horse's stall. He had been throwing corn to work horses. Neither the father nor son saw Mary. There was a car parked in the barn and she had crawled into the driver's seat, her hands on the steering wheel, pretending she was driving.

"Well," the father said. If he felt triumphant, he did not show his feeling.

"Well," said the son, "I have come back."

"Yes, I see," the father said. "They are cutting corn." He walked toward the barn door and then stopped. "It will be yours soon now," he said. "You can be boss then."

He said no more and both men went away, the father toward the distant fields and the son toward the house. Mary was afterwards quite sure that nothing more was ever said.

What had the father meant?

"When it is yours you can be boss." It was too

much for the child. Knowledge comes slowly. It meant:

"You will be in command, and for you, in your turn, it will be necessary to assert.

"Such men as we are cannot fool with delicate stuff. Some men are meant to command and others must obey. You can make them obey in your turn.

"There is a kind of death.

"Something in you must die before you can possess and command."

There was, so obviously, more than one kind of death. For Don Grey one kind and for the younger brother Ted, soon now perhaps, another.

Mary ran out of the barn that day, wanting eagerly to get out into the light, and afterwards, for a long time, she did not try to think her way through what had happened. She and her brother Ted did, however, afterwards, before he died, discuss quite often the two trees. They went on a cold day and put their fingers on the stumps, but the stumps were cold. Ted kept asserting that only men got their legs and arms cut off, and she protested. They continued doing things that had been forbidden Ted to do, but no one protested, and, a year or two later, when he died, he died during the night in his bed.

But while he lived, there was always, Mary

afterwards thought, a curious sense of freedom, something that belonged to him that made it good, a great happiness, to be with him. It was, she finally thought, because having to die his kind of death, he never had to make the surrender his brother had made—to be sure of possessions, success, his time to command—would never have to face the more subtle and terrible death that had come to his older brother.